# Solace

## by

## Gini Rifkin

*Fae Warriors, Book 1*

**Solace**

Cover Art by *Debbie Taylor*

The Wild Rose Press, Inc.
PO Box 708
Adams Basin, NY 14410-0708
Visit us at www.thewildrosepress.com

Publishing History
First Fantasy Rose Edition, 2015
Print ISBN 978-1-5092-0261-4
Digital ISBN 978-1-5092-0262-1

*Fae Warriors, Book 1*
Published in the United States of America

**"I mean it, Solace. What's going on?**
Who do you really work for?"

She opened her mouth then closed it, and those lips he coveted flattened into a line of determination barring words she seemed to be fighting to hold back.

"If you have to ask, I can't tell you," she finally said, her gaze searching his face as if she sought some grand truth, her expression almost one of pain. "I really do need to see everything."

Tanner balled his hands into fists, trying to keep his cool. Accustomed to giving orders, blindly taking them went against the grain. It went against his instincts. It went against his training. What if she were lying? The stuff she was about to see was beyond top secret. It was experimental, and in the wrong hands, it could bring down an entire country.

"Please," she said.

Although unspoken, the words *trust me* seemed to fill the space between them.

"It truly is important," she added.

Tanner stepped in front of her. She didn't blink or flinch, but rather she calmly returned his malevolent glare, the one he'd perfected to scare his worst combat enemies. Her show of toughness turned him on. And friend or enemy, he wanted her—right here, right now. He eased closer, his body pressing hers back against the wall. Recollections of being with her at the party and the stolen kisses on her balcony flooded his mind. "Are you remembering what we shared that night?" he asked.

In answer to his question, a hint of a smile curved those luscious lips. "Business first," she whispered, against his cheek. "I promise it will be worth the wait."

# Praise for Gini Rifkin

"*IRON HEART* gives the classic epic adventures a run for their money."

*~Sizzling Hot Books (5 Hearts)*

~*~

"The chemistry between these two excellent characters [in *SPECIAL DELIVERY*] is riveting. You won't want to miss finding out what happens to them."

*~Fall Into Reading Review(5 Stars)*

~*~

"Rifkin's novel [*LADY GALLANT*] is epic in scope, meticulously researched and finely detailed. A genuinely sweet romance married to an exciting war/espionage story."

*~Romantic Times Book Reviews*

~*~

[*THE DRAGON AND THE ROSE*] is an *enchanting* story!"

*~The Long and Short Review*

~*~

"[*VICTORIAN DREAM* was] written with a rich depth of detail. Nicely spiced with an underlying sense of mystery and danger."

*~Night Owl Reviews*

~*~

"[*A COWBOY'S FATE* is] a fun and entertaining story with a picturesque setting. Romance, drama, and adventure rolled into one. I was disappointed when the story ended because I wanted the journey to continue. A must read."

*~Still Moments Magazine (5 Stars)*

## Dedications

Dedicated to Kathy and Steve.
What would I do without you guys?
~*~
With special thanks to The Wild Rose Press,
and the amazing Amanda Barnett.

## Author's Note

A glossary of terms is found after page 225.

*After the Great War between the Tuatha de Danaan and the original earthlings called Milesians, the Fae were condemned to spend their lives underground. They grew smaller in stature, built magical cities in hills and burrows, and only returned to the real world after Man's belief in them had waned to the point where they could only be seen by children.*

*One tribe, however, could not abide this subterranean existence. They languished to near extinction, and Mother Nature grieved as this clan began to fade from the Earth. To save her beautiful Fae creatures, she spirited this special group to a tranquil planet in the Centaurus galaxy. Here they thrived, honing their physical skills and magical powers. With each generation, they grew larger and more fearless, becoming the most respected soldiers within five-hundred mega light years. They are The Fae Warriors—guardians of the Multiverse.*

Chapter One

*Present day Earth, Boulder, Colorado*

Solace hesitated at the door to the warehouse. Although midmorning, the inside appeared darker than a Zarminian cave.

Slipping her hand inside her purse, she wrapped her fingers around the familiar grip of her particle laser. She truly hadn't thought she'd need a weapon just to meet a client, but thank goodness she hadn't left it back at her apartment. After seeing this place, doing so could have been a big mistake.

Kind of an out-of-the-way setting for an appointment. Still, the man's claim about having a safe method of recycling mercury light bulbs sounded legit. And pretending to be the owner of an environmental research agency, she supposed these kinds of scenarios were bound to come up.

Stepping over the threshold, she sniffed the air. It smelled okay.

"Glad you could accommodate meeting me here, Miss Goodeve."

She spun around in time to see a man materialize out of the shadows.

"Mr. White. It's awfully dark in here. Could we turn on a light or step outside?"

He didn't answer but strode forward. For an instant

she thought his eyes flashed red. It couldn't be. There were a few Tuatara Reptiles known to be in the area, but the odds of meeting one in a situation like this seemed almost astronomical.

With her hand still concealed within her purse, she tightened her grip on the laser and clicked off the safety. Reptilian or not, something fishy was definitely going on here.

The man's tongue flicked out, snaking across a row of pointy teeth filling his ever-widening grin.

Crap...he *was* a Rep.

They circled one another as Mr. White's outer image dematerialized, exposing his true form. Although the Reptilian invaders had a serum capable of making them appear human, she hadn't been informed they could change at will. Gruesome as it was to watch, she couldn't look away.

His skin thickened and turned a sickly green, and his fingernails elongated. While remaining upright, he grew taller. Then his face morphed into a lizard head—creating an image only a mother could love and a dinosaur recognize.

"After I kill you," he growled, "I'm going to eat you. A little buff-Fae, if you will."

She'd been made. How had he tracked her down—known she was Fae? To ask would be pointless, reasoning with him an even bigger waste of time. Reps weren't known for deep logic.

Heart racing, stomach in a knot, she inched around a rusted-out car chassis. Where were her sisters? She tried summoning them but got no response. She couldn't even feel them. It seemed as if they were still a world away. She was on her own.

The Rep's tail, now visible, grew longer, a lethal weapon unto itself. One well-placed slash across the throat or chest, and she'd be lizard chow.

Jerking the laser free, she dropped her handbag to the ground, crouched low, and took evasive action. For a moment, the Rep appeared uncertain. The Fae Warriors had been using this weapon for over a year, yet the Rep acted surprised to see it. He quickly recovered his bravado however, and with an angry hiss, lunged forward.

She fired. The blast hit his shoulder, and a sizzling noise filled the air, followed by the smell of meat cooking. The wound barely slowed him down. This was the first Reptilian she'd faced in combat. Her tactical training insured she could hold her own anytime, anyplace. But the psychological effect of confronting a beast who wore scaly body armor like a three piece suit, and outweighed her by two hundred pounds constituted another matter altogether.

The Rep's tail whipped around, coming straight at her. She did a tuck and roll. Not quick enough. The disgusting appendage barely grazed the top of her head, still it burned like fire. Energized by the pain, she rounded on him, blasting away at his injured shoulder. His arm came off, and with a howl of rage and pain, he clamped his remaining hand over the gaping wound, green blood flowing in rivulets between his clawed fingers. If he lived, he could re-grow the arm. Frigging Reptiles could regenerate every appendage except their heads.

Pinned down beneath an overhang, she glanced around, seeking a more tactical position. Being on the defense sucked and wouldn't likely win her a way out of this mess. She needed room to maneuver and activate her battle-wings. If she could get some altitude, she could take the offensive.

While Mr. White momentarily agonized over his missing arm, she crawled to one side, then flash-moved toward the center of the high beamed building. He caught sight of the movement and lashed out again with his tail, this time smacking her flat across the back. The ground rose up to meet her as searing pain shot through her wingports. Skidding and sliding across the dirt floor, she ricocheted off a jumble of tire chains and rusted engine parts, the far wall abruptly ending her trajectory.

Scrambling to a kneeling position, she searched for her enemy. Twenty yards away and closing fast. The deadly intent in his cold black eyes chilled her to the core. Thank Jupiter she'd managed to keep a grip on her laser. Fingers trembling, she set it to maximum load. Would one blast do the job? There'd be no second chances; it would drain her weapon, leaving her armed with only her good looks and charming personality.

"Dinner is served," he roared, lips curled back, teeth exposed.

"Eat this you mutated bastard," she yelled, squeezing the trigger.

**** 

Solace lay on her back staring up at the warehouse ceiling. Her right arm slid off her chest and flopped down at her side, and her fingers uncurled from the grip of the now useless particle laser.

Breathing in fits and starts, she tried once more to summon Portence and Bliss. Still no response. If ever she needed her sisters, it was now. Where were they?

why didn't they answer?

Her head hurt like Hades, and she felt weak, so weak. The light in her soul flickered, and she knew for one brief second, the light in the realm from which she came dimmed. Forcing herself to take slow deep breaths, she lay still, listening for signs of life around her. It was quiet as deep space. Apparently no one had heard the commotion—one lucky break at least.

Fracturing the silence, a boisterous pair of pigeons flew in through the open warehouse doors. She jolted at the unexpected ruckus then groaned as the movement sent waves of pain raging through her muscles. The rambunctious feathered couple settled up in the rafters, sending a spate of dust and dirt drifting downward.

Her body felt as if it weighed a cosmic ton, and it took a monumental effort just to raise her head a few inches to glance around. Obviously her business meeting had been a trap. The Fae-eater had been waiting for her.

The Reps mission was to take over the earth, destroying anything and anyone who got in their way. Her mission, destroy them first. A smile of satisfaction twisted across her battered face. At least this Reptilian would never kill another of her kind.

The scaly wretch's body, lay ten feet away, his decapitated head another five. Green blood ran everywhere, and a rotten sulfuric odor poisoned the air making her stomach heave. Alive or dead, those second cousins to lizards could emit a stench wretched enough to make your eyes water. At least they usually did—but she hadn't smelled this one until she'd wounded him. Another new trick in the Reptilian repertoire?

Gritting her teeth, she rolled sideways and grappled

up onto her hands and knees. Body shaking, head hanging, she waited for the world to stop spinning. After a few more deep breaths, her heart rate slowed, and she felt less like puking. Maybe she wasn't hurt as seriously as she thought. One thing for sure, she had to get back to her apartment, had to contact Mother, and find out what was going on. She'd been careful. How the heck had a Rep ferreted out her location?

****

One hot shower and two diet sodas later, she felt almost human, the very idea making her smile. She would never wish to be anything other than Fae; and with all the entities in the Multiverse from which to choose, surely not a human. Still, years and years of Earth Indoctrination Training had left slang and colloquialisms ingrained in her psyche and oftentimes tumbling from her lips.

Naked as a cherub, she wandered into the bedroom. Holy Cassiopeia—she should have avoided the full-length mirror. Actually seeing the new war wounds made her hurt all the more. Gritting her teeth, she gathered aside her hair to reveal a myriad of cuts and bruises scattered up and down the length of her body. On the plus side, her henna tribal tattoos helped to hide some of the purple and red markings on her chest. Thank goodness she hadn't needed stitches.

Reporting to the local ER would be a disaster. Faes had a different chemistry than humans, were susceptible to different diseases, and they had blue blood. She'd been warned not to visit any medical facilities other than the ones Mother Nature had set up especially designated for her kind, and only if the situation appeared life or death. Fortunately, that hadn't been the case today.

Turning, she glanced over her shoulder, checking out her wingports. They hurt like crazy. Not being able to fly or transport had been a tricky business. On the taxi ride home, she'd had to talk fast to convince the cabbie the blue and green stains on her clothing were merely the result of being the biggest loser ever in a paintball war game.

She tried again but couldn't even pull-off a simple levitation, the effort hurting her ports with renewed vigor. What if they were permanently damaged? The thought of never flying again made her dizzy, the idea too awful to contemplate. If things didn't clear up, she really would need to go to the clinic.

With a sigh, she released the clutch of hair. It cascaded around her like her favorite black shawl, hiding the damaged flesh as the ends licked the tender skin at the small of her back. Then she sank down onto the edge of her bed. What a less than stellar beginning to her first assignment on Earth. And where the heck was everybody? Why hadn't they called? She'd left a message at headquarters twenty minutes ago. It seemed like hours.

When the phone rang, she gingerly gained her feet, and limped toward the long awaited sound.

"Mother, thank goodness. What happened? I never even smelled him."

"I'm sorry, Solace. We've only just learned the Reps have developed a medication which alters their odor. From the beginning, this has been one of their top research projects, and with several Big Pharmas under their thumb, it's finally been realized. I take it you suffered no permanent injuries?"

"Nothing that won't mend, I hope. But I'm not able to fly, and you know how I hate using normal transportation."

Mother chuckled. "Yes. Almost as much as you hate having only humans with whom to couple."

Heat warmed her cheeks. Sometimes Mother knew too much. "It won't happen again," she said, and meant it.

"Yes it will. You're a hot blooded Fae female, and I'm afraid it's all part of the package. Just remember—even when you're between the sheets, you're still undercover."

"Yes, Mother."

Between the sheets, a lovely phrase triggering a remembered wanting. Then sadness washed the image away. A little over a year ago, her Fae lover, Duncan, had been killed, and the memory of their last time together remained a heartbreaking comfort. No species, Fae or otherwise, had ever so deeply touched her. As warriors, they all knew death might find them, but losing Duncan hurt more than she ever imagined it could. She had loved him with all her heart.

Besides, her unplanned one-night-stand two weeks ago had just been sex, not making love, and it made her sad not happy. For once Mother might be wrong. It would take someone incredibly special to make her want to scratch that itch again.

"Are you listening," Mother scolded.

"Yes, no, what? Bad connection here."

"Bad connection my asteroids. I don't have bad connections. I'm not even using a phone. Really Solace, I know you're only two-hundred years old, a mere child in the scheme of things, but you must try to keep on track. After today, I'm sure you fully realize we're in a life or death struggle. Our operatives, as well as the Earthlings, are in jeopardy until we eradicate these Tuatara Reptiles. And it's taking longer than expected. They're more deeply entrenched than we suspected, and more scientifically advanced than we were led to believe."

"Sorry, I'm listening. I'm tired and still feeling woozy." Her head pounded anew, and she still ached all over. "Did you find out how he knew about me? I've been careful, and when he made contact before the meeting, he knew all the right answers about our burgeoning agency."

"The Reptilians are making inroads in all areas," her superior said, dancing around a direct answer. "Other than their eyes occasionally flashing red, they're beginning to look as normal as any human. Worse yet, they have a number of new field operatives. They're scattered all across the country, making containment difficult. They're even lurking throughout the ranks of the Federal Government—including Homeland Security. It makes our ability to halt their invasion harder by the day. Which is the reason I'm relying heavily upon you and your sisters."

"Then how come I can't get in touch with Bliss and Portence? You said they were Earth-side."

"There's been a delay. I needed them to verify a few things on their way there. The Reps are frightfully close to attaining nuclear weaponry, and they're experimenting with controlling the weather. Scuttlebutt has it they're hoping to infiltrate NOAA, the National Oceanic and Atmospheric Administration."

"I know what it is," Solace interrupted, "the place

is located right here in Boulder. Is that why we're to be stationed here?"

"Yes, one of the reasons. It will no doubt be high on their list of targets."

"Sounds reasonable, but what about my sisters?" Boy, sometimes you just had to keep pounding away to get a straight answer out of Mother.

"When you tried to reach your sisters, they were in the outer realms, correlating a firsthand account of NOAA's satellites, both geostationary and polar operational. They're also taking a visual of the deserts in the southwest, checking for hotspots indicating any unauthorized bomb testing."

"You mean they were completely out of communication range for an extended amount of time?" Not a good situation. "That's dangerous for them. And," she dared to add, "I could have dang-well used their help today."

"As soon as they're back on terra firma and debriefed, I'll send them along to you. Your being caught without backup won't happen again. With the three of you working together, you'll have safety in numbers. Of course," she added with emphasis, "my expectations will be all the greater—and no shenanigans like last time."

Geez would they never live down one childish indiscretion? "We've all been good as Caronium gold since then," she pointed out.

"I know. I've been keeping a close watch on all three of you ladies. If nothing else, your prior escapade proved instrumental in deciding your futures and the course of your educations. And because the three of you have shown great promise as warriors, the previous black mark has been expunged from each of your records."

What an unexpected gift—she could hardly wait to tell the others. "Thank you, Mother, it means a great deal to all of us. So, how did the Rep find me?"

Mother hesitated, and Solace knew she wasn't going to like the answer.

"We had a breach of security. One of your own kind."

Stunned, Solace felt first disbelief then anger. The Faes had struggled hard to become respected citizens and guardians of the Multiverse. Their solidarity and code of honor ranked the highest in any realm. It sickened her to think such a thing possible.

"Power and greed can corrupt even the best of us," Mother said gently, as if she knew the heartache her words had wrought. "Generally speaking, that's exactly what is wrong with this planet, and why it's heading for a downfall unheard of in modern times."

"You caught the traitor?"

"Yes. He's been outcast to Rigel 5, with no reprieve."

Although the turncoat deserved what he got, the idea of being sent to Rigel 5 sent a shiver through her. A cold dark planet, it had a gravitational force so strong it prohibited flying. With the food source extremely limited, and the predatory species plentiful, living there would be a nightmare. The daily challenge of staying alive an option one might disregard after a while, with death coming as a relief.

"You'll need to move out of your apartment," Mother instructed, bringing Solace back to the present. "It's too risky for you to stay there now. Besides, I want all of you girls under one roof. I'll messenger over your info packets and the keys to your new place. Now go rest. I'm glad you weren't mortally wounded."

"Thank y—" A burst of static cut her short. Evidently Mother had "disconnected".

Solace smiled. Quite the surprise for Mother to offer gratitude for the fact she hadn't been killed. It seemed almost downright sentimental, not Mother's normal tough-love strategy.

Solace clicked off her handheld, and at the thought of seeing her sisters, she joyfully spun around quickly regretting the sudden movement. Her body still demanded she tread lightly, but her heart and soul were doing cartwheels anticipating the long awaited reunion.

Separation from one another had been the worst part of their punishment. But she'd learned her lesson well. You really couldn't fool Mother Nature. And if you were dumb enough to try, the repercussions could literally be out of this world.

While estranged, all three sisters had attained combatant status, not a trivial achievement. Yet even after becoming Warriors, they had been given separate assignments, their missions spanning many universes and dimensions. Now they would be reunited, assigned to battle the Outerworld's latest plan to wreak havoc on Earth, and their training and kick-ass exuberance would finally be put to good use as a team.

She headed for the bedroom, stepping around two unopened trunks. At least moving to their new location presented no problem. Her arrival on Earth had been so recent, she hadn't unpacked what few items she'd brought along. With a yawn, she gave a cautious stretch and eased down onto the bed. Zowns, she was tired. A quick nap sounded heavenly.

****

Mother Nature relaxed upon her fainting couch, glad Solace sounded safe and not seriously injured. It had been difficult not to overindulge her with sympathy, but warriors had to be tough or they wouldn't survive the chaos conjured by the baser entities existing in so many forms.

She couldn't help but smile. When the three sisters were united, they'd be hell on wheels. And that's just what she needed to save this planet. Earth was one of her favorites, but she was disappointed with the path the humans had chosen to follow. They were horribly materialistic, taking for granted the world they'd inherited.

She shook her head at the sadness of it all. Over the eons, the humans had remained childlike, endearing in their playfulness, but totally thoughtless and completely egotistical in their belief they were the only intelligent species. Their arrogance continued to ruin the planet, blinding them to the very danger lurking in their midst. Without intervention, this would surely be the beginning of the end for them. Maybe even the end of this sector of the galaxy.

Perhaps the fault lay with her. She had been too lenient with the human creatures. Oh sure, she sent them warnings—worldwide flooding, the black plague, the sinking of Atlantis, and other lesser heads-up. But they just didn't get it. They killed more of each other in wars and from pollution then the tolls taken by her earthquakes and volcanic eruptions combined. Now, as this new enemy loomed on their horizon, bringing her Fae Warriors here to help seemed the only viable answer, albeit a drastic and rarely used measure.

Too bad only her female troops were available, the male Fae being occupied on Cronos 12. This divided her boots on the ground—or rather her wings in the air. And although she had complete faith in her female warriors, fighting Fae-eating Reps could be tricky. She would have been happier going into this with all troops available.

Fortunately, the Reps were arriving in small clusters, and if thwarted quickly, her numbers would suffice. The smile returned to her face. Things were going to get interesting.

Chapter Two

Solace ambled around the penthouse apartment, her four-inch heels clicking on the hardwood floors. Mother had spared no expense. All just part of their cover she supposed, but perhaps also an apology for the pounding Solace had taken. Whatever the reason, it was fantastic, and more than she expected.

There were three bedrooms and three bathrooms, which should cut down on the "infighting," a fireplace, and a gourmet kitchen. Beautifully furnished, it was enough to make a metrosexual weep.

Sliding open the double glass doors, she stepped out onto the wrap-around balcony, checked the temperature of the hot tub, and cranked the setting higher. The soothing heat would feel good later. Then she stood gazing at the foothills of the Rocky Mountains. In the late afternoon sun, the Flat Irons appeared purple. The stunning vista made her wish to launch herself off the top rail to revel in the view from an even higher perspective. But flying remained out of the question and still a concern. What would she do if she could never fly again? Best not to go there.

Before the buzzer sounded, she turned and hurried toward the front door. It had to be her sisters, she could feel their auras. Swinging wide the door, they fell into one another's arms. They were triplets, and except for their concept of the ideal man, their preferred weapon of choice, and the color of their hair, they were mirror images of one another.

They had been born far away on a very different planet, but during their extended training, they'd lived right here on Earth, home of their ancestors. And back then, they were always together, if you found one, you found all three. Their strong spiritual connection, limited only by distance, had always been a comfort. Being separated had been a terribly hurtful punishment. Fortunately, in preparation for reuniting, they had been allowed to text communicate, catching up and reconnecting on *Spacebook*, the Outerworld's version of Facebook. Now, arms wrapped around one another, they danced in a circle, laughing with glee.

"I've missed you guys so much." The words echo simultaneously from all three.

"Ouch." Solace grimaced as Bliss touched a hyper-sore area on her back.

Bliss jerked her hand away. "I'm sorry. You're not really all right, are you? Mother told us what happened." Bliss nudged Solace away from the foyer and toward the overstuffed sofa. Among the three of them, Bliss was the most nurturing. She shook her head in concern, sending a ripple through her reddish-gold hair. "You should sit down."

"I'm fine," Solace fibbed, refusing to dampen the reunion.

"We've been so worried," Portence called over her shoulder as she closed the apartment door. "Glad you off'd that Rep bastard," she added, with a growl and a toss of pure white mane. "I'm proud of you sis."

Rather than lounging in the living area, Solace ushered her sisters toward the kitchen. "He put up a good fight, and morphed right before my eyes. It was gross. And to be honest, wet-your-pants scary."

"What did you do to tip him off you were Fae?" Portence asked, assuming her infuriating older sister expression which really meant *how'd you screw up this time*.

Age-wise, only a matter of minutes determined the sister's pecking order, but Portence never missed an opportunity to press home the fact she held the eldest position. She was also the toughest, and bossiest, but generally right. Solace, the impulsive peacekeeper, claimed the middle rank, leaving compassion and mind-melding with animals to "baby" Bliss.

"I didn't do anything," Solace stubbornly replied. "He found me because a Fae traitor infiltrated Mother's ranks."

Just as she had been, both her sisters appeared stunned at the revelation.

"Liar," Portence said, refusing to believe such terrible news.

"I know it doesn't seem possible, but the info came straight from Mother. There'd be no purpose in her making up something so horrible. That means," Solace emphasized, "we can't trust anyone accept each other."

Her sisters stood in silence, trying to absorb the disturbing information.

"Hey, are you hungry?" she asked, hoping to restore their former happiness. "The fridge is fully stocked, and I already made a pitcher of margaritas."

For some reason, no matter the season, this drink had always appealed to all three of them. Salty and cool, citrus and tangy it went down easy. Being Fae, they had an unusually large capacity for drinking alcoholic beverages with little effect. A great advantage on a date, still with serious diligence they could manage a healthy buzz.

"I'm in." Portence grinned, flopping into a chair at the table.

"Me too." Bliss followed suite, in a much more ladylike manner.

Rummaging around in the cupboard, Solace found appropriate glasses. After salting the rims, she set them on the table with the full pitcher.

Allowing Bliss to pour, Solace handed out three manila envelopes delivered a short while ago from headquarters. "Here are the details on our cover story."

They all took a hearty sip and sat staring at the folders awaiting their perusal.

"Not down to business already," Portence protested. "My mind's in a whirl. I'm still fighting warp-lag."

"Well, we do have a lot to make up for," Bliss pointed out, "and we can't mess up again. There's a great deal for which we must atone."

"What a load of cosmic crap," Portence snapped back. "We've all paid ten times over for one prankish infraction. Mother just has us brainwashed into thinking it's the worst debacle in Fae history. That way she can keep us on a short leash and boss us around."

"Take it easy, Port," Solace interrupted. "You'll both be happy to know, the whole affair has been expunged from our records."

"It's about time," Portence said, with a harrumph. "Who would have thought one little unicorn could cause so much trouble."

A collective giggle echoed in the room quickly

turning into full-fledged laughter. Bliss pounded the table with her open palm. "Oh, Mars bars." She gasped, which for her was as close to cussing as she ever came. "Remember the look on the humans' faces. It was priceless."

On a Midsummer's Eve, during their Earth Indoctrination, the triplets had become bored with sprinkling faery dust on moonbeams and retrieving teeth from beneath children's pillows. So, they went rogue, flying off to Stonehenge where they turned a unicorn loose right in the middle of a Twentieth Century Wicca ceremony. Panic had ensued. And the crowd-control police, definitely out of their league when it came to rounding up unicorns, radioed for a swat team.

"You're the one who caused the military to get involved," Solace reminded Bliss. "If you hadn't floated the cavorting beast up into the ether, they wouldn't have mistaken him for an intercontinental ballistic missile."

"I was afraid he might be hurt," Bliss defended.

"England thought Russia had launched an ICBM." Portence laughed. "When they were about to retaliate, we were definitely screwed. Mother's temper flared so hot I thought her head would explode. Lucky for us, she took out the majority of her anger on a passing asteroid."

Bliss clapped her hands at the memory. "Oh yes, the meteor shower. A beautiful and perfect diversion. Unfortunately it terrified the humans. But what really saved the day was when Mother fouled-up the British homeland security instruments."

"She's pretty darn good at creative thinking on the

fly," Solace agreed.

"I felt sorry for the poor Wiccans," Bliss mused. "How unfair they were written off as crazies, going on and on about the unicorn. Unfair, but it helped save our butts."

"Only momentarily," Portence reminded. "I still say Mother overreacted. I sure never dreamed she would be so cruel as to separate us. But I guess all's well, that ends well."

"But it isn't the end, Port," Solace declared. "It's just the beginning. A lot has changed in the near half-century we've been gone. Aren't you guys excited to be assigned to Earth to battle the Reps?" She reached for the pitcher of Margaritas, which set her shoulder to throbbing and taking a bit of edge off her swagger. "But remember," she warned, ignoring the pain as best she could, "since we can't smell them now until they're dead or wounded, our enemy is even more dangerous. An unexpected disadvantage."

"I'm definitely anxious to use my new skills," Bliss agreed. "Learning Fae martial arts from a Dagda descendent had always been a dream of mine. And these days, Master Abbadon rarely takes on new students. Although I have to admit, being his first female student had its ups and downs. It frosted the male Faes, prompting bruised egos and numerous practical jokes."

"Bet they thawed quickly enough," Port jibed. "Your best weapon will always be your uncanny ability to render men senseless just by looking at them.

"It does come in handy," Bliss admitted, with an unabashed grin. "And speaking of men, have you had any yet, Sol."

"Criminy Dutch, Bliss, I've only been here two weeks."

"And?"

"Okay, just one. I found it unfulfilling. The man tried, but being earthbound it's just not the same as sky-riding with a hot Fae lover."

"I refuse to mate with an Earthling," Portence declared. "I'll either go without, or manage things myself."

"I've been told Earth men are rather sweet," Bliss defended. "Male Faes can be so egotistical, and not very sensitive. Except for Duncan, of course," she added. "We all liked Duncan, Sol."

Solace nodded. "He was special. I still miss him a lot."

"You always will," Bliss said patting her sister's outstretched hand. "It's not something you get over, just something at some point you must get on with."

A piece of her heart would always belong to Duncan. But as the life expectancy of a Fae could be quite extensive, unlike Portence, she couldn't imagine "going without" for an extended period of time. Besides, Duncan always knew she was a randy little Fae, he wouldn't expect her to be celibate.

"Let's check out what Mother gave us," Solace suggested, wanting to change the subject. She'd been given a prelim rundown, but the info in the packets would be new to her sisters.

They tore open the envelopes, scanning the enclosures.

"Our last name is Goodeve?" Portence said. "What a hoot."

"Isn't Goodeve a woman's hygiene product?" Bliss

asked, wide-eyed.

"Close, but no," Solace reassured.

"And we're to run an environmental research agency called Green Goddess," Portence murmured.

"I like that idea." Bliss smiled. "We can make a difference even with our fake jobs."

"I have to interview some guy named Tanner Jackson." Solace sighed, studying her material. "He works for NOAA. Probably some little pencil pusher with thick glasses and no sense of humor."

"Stop whining, it could be worse. Bliss and I are supposed to rent office space, set up the computers, and backlog a database of nonexistent clients. That should be loads of fun."

She granted Portence a sympathetic look. While Solace favored Earth's nineteenth and twentieth century time periods, Port loved the historical eras, had no interest in computers, and tended to live by the old Fae philosophies. Bliss liked modern day gadgets and finding out what made things work.

Personally, Solace would rather blow things up than delve into their construction, but she'd have to discover what made Tanner Jackson tick. Mother mentioned the Reps were interested in NOAA, which meant her interview with this guy would be more than a superficial fact finding mission. Building contacts with various top companies in the community would be helpful, but getting eyes and ears inside this organization might turn out to be crucial.

"Enough about work," Portence declared. "We can study the details tomorrow. The sun has set and I'm starving. I say we build a few celestial sub sandwiches, whip up another pitcher of margaritas, and hit the hot tub.

By mutual agreement, all three jumped up, and headed for the kitchen. Within minutes, their feast awaited on the balcony, and without a second thought, they shed their clothes and slipped into the steaming water.

"Oh, Solace," Bliss gasped. "You really took a beating. I've some Saturnalia cream with me. We'll put some on you after we soak."

Portence also winced. "It's going to be a pleasure busting the balls of these scaly scumbags," she fumed. "Mother said your wingports were out of commission. Are they any better?"

"They don't hurt as much, but I haven't even dared to try creation mode, so flying is still definitely out. At this point, I don't think I could even conjure party wings."

Depending on the situation, Faes had a variety of wing types from which to choose. An extensive selection actually—from frothy designer creations, including custom colors and sparkles, to full-fledged iron-spiked combat ready. Too bad rules and regs while on Earth restricted when and where they could summon and use them.

Glancing back through the sliding glass doors, Solace's gaze fell on her purse hanging from the back of a chair. "Darn, I left my particle laser in my bag. It needs recharging. The thing weighs so much I nearly left it home when I went to the warehouse. If I had," she emphasized, "I'd be dead. We mustn't go anywhere without them."

"Is there a charger in the apartment?" Portence asked.

"One in each of our bedrooms. Don't forget to use it before turning in tonight. You did bring your weapons, right?"

"We did, plus Port sent the usual archaic arsenal on ahead," Bliss teased. "Crossbow, garrote, slingshot, atlatl."

"An atlatl." Solace nodded her approval. "Nice choice. One step up from a spear, yet not as fussy as a bow and arrow. Can't scoff at a weapon dating all the way back to 15,000 B.C."

"It never hurts to be diversified," Port defended. "Besides, not all weapons have to make an explosion to be effective. I dream of one day owning a trebuchet."

"I don't think it would fit on the balcony," Solace said, with a laugh.

"Sorry we weren't there for you sis," Port added, her face serious. "Things will be different from now on."

Being among the youngest members of the Fae Warrior Alpha Sector, the three of them were also deemed the wildest, or as Solace preferred to think of it, the most energetic. No one cut her any slack because of her age, and she didn't want any. The other operatives were older and more experienced, but the three of them were just as good—maybe better—and definitely anxious to make their bones in real-life experience here on earth. They'd already proven themselves elsewhere. And based on today's activities, they wouldn't have long to wait for opportunities to show what they could do.

"A toast," Portence said. "To Mother, for bringing us back together again."

"To Mother," they cheered in unison.

"And," Solace added, "for our chance to kick butt and show what we've learned.

"To the power of three," they chanted, "so shall it be."

\*\*\*\*

They told war stories from their exploits, and laughed until their cheeks hurt. Then the sky eased from navy blue to inky black, and the stars winked on. Before long, travel time and the margaritas caught up with Port and Bliss and they turned in.

Alone in the night, Solace floated in the water, marveling at how far they had come. They were full-grown warrior women now, no longer prankish teenagers. And geographically speaking, they had traveled the galaxy, and seen civilizations struggling to survive at all stages of evolutionary development.

Along the way, each had made friends with species beyond the imagining of the humans. And spiritually, they now returned to their roots, an arduous journey, yet she felt pride in her accomplishments, knew her sisters did too.

Their basic training had included history—fifteen hundred years' worth. At first, her rebellious nature rejected learning about the past, but hearing in detail the hardships faced by her forefathers, her indifference had changed to pride and curiosity.

Originally, her ancestors had lived a magical life in the Fair Isles. They were the Tuatha de Danann, the people of the Goddess Danu. And being the offspring of the fallen angels, the Anunnaki, they were also known as The Dragon Lords of Anu.

Back then, they roamed freely across the land—until the war with the Milesians. These forerunners of the Irish people defeated the Fae, driving them to the underworld, forcing them to live in hills and barrows. Some of the Fae could not bear this fate, so Mother had taken those who wished to go to another world. There they could live in peace above ground with one stipulation. Each generation must return to Earth for the mandatory homeland training, which is when Solace and her sisters had run amuck.

As the centuries passed, the Fae from her tribe grew larger and more skilled, especially in self-defense and warfare. They no longer coveted the Earth, and they were here now only at Mother's bidding. How ironic to be charged with the task of covertly helping the humans whose forbearers had once banished them. Nothing like a mutual enemy to bring previously feuding folks together.

The Reptiles had a long history as well, one of being hated and feared throughout time. And although the older Fae had locked horns with them in days-gone-by, somehow this felt like a final showdown. The Fae were ready. They were no longer fragile beings once believed-in only by human children. They were Mother Nature's finest, a force with which to be reckoned—the Earth's only hope.

Chapter Three

Joe Smith locked the door, crossed the room, and stood staring out the window of his eighth floor office. Situated in the tallest building in Boulder, he could see the hustle and bustle of Pearl Street Mall one block away, as well as the foothills a bit farther to the west.

What a beautiful sight in the midday sun. He wondered how much, if any of it would survive the insurrection. Sacrifices always had to be made—destruction a necessary part of the plan.

Easing a fine linen handkerchief from the breast pocket of his suit, he dabbed at the spittle leaking from the corner of his mouth. He needed a fix. Stepping away from the window, he entered the small sitting area and glanced at his image in the mirror.

The human form reflected back wavered, stretched thin like a hologram. When he blinked, the nictitating membrane usually hidden, slid across his eye then retreated. Forcing a mirthless grin, he ran his tongue over the sharp white teeth gleaming through the false image. He hated living in this ridiculous human form. He found suppressing his scaly invincible self extremely irritating, both physically and mentally.

With a grumble, he opened the wall safe and removed the satchel containing the pre-loaded syringes of serum that would halt his *turning*. Selecting one, he slipped off the cap to expose the needle then plunged it into the side of his neck. It didn't hurt, his nervous system being less sensitive than a puny human's, or Humes as Out-worlders referred to them. The Humes were weak, they didn't deserve to rule the earth—and soon they wouldn't.

He relaxed, issued a groan of surrender, and let the transformation slip over him. His claw-tipped fingernails retreated, and his emerging reptilian body began to compress, it felt as if he were being stuffed into clothing two sizes too small. Now he would again look like any normal man. Apparently a rather good-looking one, or so he'd been told by the Earth females. He couldn't really tell. To him all male Humes were ugly with their thin skin, flimsy bodies, and squeaky voices.

The females were nice and soft though, but mating with them presented a problem. So far, bringing forth a new race of crossbreeds had yet to be attained outside the laboratory, and even then, not always with success.

The serum in the Reptilian injections replicated the best physical human traits, and it converted all the Reptilian external features with pinpoint accuracy, accept one, their genitalia. This area remained large by human standards, and thorny. Copulating with human females always ended in disaster as he literally screwed them to death. He didn't feel any remorse for the situation, but it was bloody inconvenient, in more ways than one. After the first few, he'd had to be more careful. Now, slaking his urges meant selecting only females who wouldn't be missed, such as prostitutes, or the women sent to him by the task force. A situation barely enough to keep him satisfied.

To date, no female Reptilians were allowed to

roam on Earth. The Big Pharmas hadn't come up with an injection to successfully convert them. Something to do with female hormones and reproductive organs being more complex. A large group of them remained in seclusion, living in the remote backcountry of New Zealand. He hoped the medical conundrum would never be resolved, hoped it would elude science forever. Reptilian women were vicious creatures, and co-existing with then proved a tiresome chore not missed by any male Tuatara he knew. He doubted the female of his species would be any nicer in human form.

Normal Reptilian procreation consisted of a clutch of eggs laid every four years, never seen again and never thought about by the males or females. No emotional attachment existed, with the young raised in groups by the Committee. He was content with the way things were. Don't fix it if it ain't broke, to quote what he'd heard one human say.

The phone on his desk beeped. His secretary must have returned from lunch. He punched the flashing button.

"Yes, Veronica."

"There's a Mr. Jones here to see you Mr. Smith. He doesn't have an appointment. Shall I buzz him in?"

"Yes. That will be fine. Thank you."

Not bothering to check the mirror to be sure the transformation was complete, or to stow the satchel and serum, he unlocked the door, then paced back and forth in front of the window. He wished it could be opened. It always seemed too hot in here. Trapped in this human costume, he felt as if he couldn't catch a decent breath. But today, more than the sunlight set his cold blood to boiling. One of their best operatives had been killed. No doubt Jones would have the full story, and delight in the telling of it. He and Jones were on equal footing in the Reptilian hierarchy, but Jones always seemed to be one step ahead in tail-kissing and information gathering.

The door opened, and Jones sauntered in, apparently even the loss of a fellow agent didn't jar his cocksure attitude. He closed the door, crossed the room, and dared to lounge one hip on the corner of the desk. *His desk, in his office.* What a profoundly irritating jerk.

"They're here, in Colorado," Jones simply said.

"Damn."

So that's what had happened. Not an accident or untoward event, a friggin' Fae had caused White's death. Winged avengers, arrogant do-gooders, the bane of Reptilian existence, even here on Earth. How he hated the Fae.

The Reps had detected the presence of a several Warriors in worldwide locations, including parts of North America, but this was the first one officially spotted in Colorado. The mountain state housed three main tactical objectives, and obtaining control of them played an instrumental part in the Reptilian takeover. Now it would be all the harder.

"I thought they were tied up fighting on Cronos 12."

"Apparently they're winning the outer-realm battle and feel they have operatives to spare. It was another female," Jones added.

"Which hardly eases my concern," Smith snapped. "Except for their size, they're every bit as dangerous as the males. Exactly what happened?"

"Agent White tracked her down through our Fae informer," Jones explained. "Who, by the way, has been found out and shuttled off to Rigel 5."

"Replacing him won't be easy," Smith groused, an agitated hiss following his words.

"Nearly impossible. Anyway, as the story goes, White reported in the night before he died, indicating he intended to lure the Fae to a warehouse and terminate her. Knowing White, his agenda probably included eating her after the kill."

Smith's stomach growled, and his mouth watered, and it took a conscious effort to stop his tongue from flicking. What he wouldn't give to capture a Fae female, and use her at his leisure.

"Sounds like he got overconfident," Smith said, trying to ignore the rush of heat in his groin, "or maybe his capabilities were weakened from having been transformed for so long. Being one of the first to arrive, he may have been suffering from side effects." A concern close to his own heart, as he had been here quite some time himself.

"All I know is there must have been one horrendous fight. And even though she couldn't smell him, once he revealed his hand, it was all over. Green blood showed everywhere, but not much of hers. And there were signs she used a particle laser gun."

"That's not possible."

"Tell that to White. It's probably what saved her ass and fried his."

"Shit."

"The blue blooded bitch relieved him of his head, eliminating any hope for regeneration."

"This is worse than I imagined. Now they know for certain we're in the vicinity, and they're armed to the teeth."

"I think they already knew we were here. Otherwise why would the old Crone send the Fae to this location?"

"Maybe just covering her bases. It's simply good strategy to have this sector secured and watched. It's valuable for their defense, as well as our offense."

"True. I guess the whys and wherefores are moot now anyway. We need to step up the timetable. And those orders came straight from the top."

"What's first," Smith asked.

"NOAA. Once our operative is inside, we can begin monitoring the planet from space. The assignment went to Thompson. He's due to arrive any day. I'll leave his bio and documentation with you so you can oversee and track his progress. He's always struck me as a bit odd, but he's the most qualified. We've already created a position for him by eliminating one of their employees. Don't hesitate to call if you have any questions."

"If I have questions, I'll call H.Q. directly. I don't need any intermediary assistance from you."

"Sure, whatever. Just offering to help."

Yeah, Smith thought, help yourself to a promotion. Always a glory boy, Jones worked hard at keeping his name and accomplishments under the noses of the higher ups. And ever since their days in military training, the competition between the two of them had been rabid. They had frequently been pitted against one another on the practice field, and sometimes things had gotten pretty rough. Back then, they had been in reptile form, and both bore scars from those encounters.

Jones retrieved several folded papers from his inside jacket pocket and with a grin, tossed them on the desk. For some reason, Jones' teeth always retained a good deal of their pointy quality, making him look more feral than most conversions.

"Keep it real," Jones quipped, over his shoulder on the way out. "And keep in touch. I'll be interested in knowing how Thompson makes out."

Yeah, Smith thought, interested in taking the credit if he succeeds. He followed Jones, stuck his head out the office door, and called to his secretary. "I don't wish to be disturbed for the next two hours."

"Yes, Mr. Smith, I'll see to it."

He closed the door and leaned back against it, his gaze sweeping the room then holding fast on the large framed photo hanging on the wall. The rendering, beautiful and powerful, depicted a male Tuatara in all his glory, *not* a lizard, although the two were often annoyingly confused. His ancestors were not lunk-headed, slithering monsters. They were the most special of all reptiles, tracing their ancestry back two-hundred million years. At one time they ran with the dinosaurs, right here on Earth. Then when extinction threatened, the last remaining few along with samples of DNA had been transferred to another planet.

Having a pelvic girdle more similar to humans than lizards, they had easily learned to walk upright. Soon after, they began to use tools, and develop a language. They formed a society, remaining hidden for centuries in the vast mountainous planet Tuata. Then rather than eating their "masters", which they could easily have done, they learned from them. The rest, as they say, is history—the future theirs for the taking. They would reclaim Earth, and as bidden, enslave or eliminate the humans.

Chapter Four

The day promised to be hot. The sky so blue it hurt her eyes to look at it. A sundress would have been a more comfortable outfit of choice, but Solace's battered body dictated she wear white Capri pants and a sheer lavender V-neck pullover. Despite Bliss' salve treatment, her cuts and bruises were frightfully obvious and would no doubt draw undue notice.

Glancing in the rearview mirror, she checked her makeup then ran her left hand down the front of her body. The silk cammie beneath her top felt deliciously soothing against her bare breasts, and the pants fit like a glove. Hey, even thwarting undue notice, a girl wanted *some* attention.

Mother had scheduled her appointment with Tanner Jackson for 10:00 AM, and she'd have to hustle to make it on time. Kicking the little crossover car into fifth gear, she headed down Canyon Drive, merged into the heavier traffic on the outskirts of Boulder, and hoped for the best.

*Broadway ¼ mile*. Good, she'd made up some time. Taking the off ramp, she turned south on the four lane street, slowed to a crawl, and began checking the addresses on the building fronts.

There, at last, the discreet blue and white sign displaying the NOAA emblem with National Geophysical Data Center in smaller print beneath it.

She'd done some prelim work on her laptop this morning and learned there were several branch headquarters besides the one in Colorado. There were offices in Maryland, Mississippi, and North Carolina—each with its own specialty. The Reps would no doubt try to embed someone in all four facilities, but the National Geophysical Data Center here in Boulder would prove especially important. NGDC worked with solar events, geomagnetic data, and earth observations from space. To control this branch would be a big plus.

She parked in the visitors' lot and gritting her teeth, gingerly climbed out of the low slung vehicle. Her muscles screamed after being stationary on the drive in. Promising herself another soak in the hot tub tonight, she grabbed her weighty purse, slipped the strap over her shoulder, and headed for the front door.

The tiny lobby offered uncomfortable looking wooden chairs and no magazines. Evidently loitering was not an event encouraged here. Even simple comfort seemed to have escaped the decorator. The unadorned beige wall across from the entrance accommodated a large unmarked door on the left, with a window beside it fitted with a counter and thick bulletproof glass.

Stepping up to the booth, she worked at being patient as she waited to be acknowledged. On the other side of the partition, a man dressed in a military-like uniform stood carefully sorting and arranging papers on his portion of the counter. What was the deal, had she gone invisible? Cripes, even in her flats she measured six feet tall, he must see her. She rapped on the glass. Without glancing up, he pointed to the clock on the wall to her right then went back to diligently sorting and shuffling papers. Nine fifty-eight. The sign below the clock boldly stated the hours open to the public were between ten o'clock and two. Talk about sticklers for punctuality. Arms folded across her chest, she stared at him wishing she possessed the power to burn a hole through glass like the yogi masters of Carpathena.

A buzzer sounded announcing the arrival of the ten o'clock hour, and the panel in the glass smoothly slid open. The man abruptly set aside his work, and gave her his full attention.

"Name please and state your business."

He scrutinized her face but didn't crack a hint of a smile.

"I'm Solace Goodeve, here to speak with Tanner Jackson."

"Identification."

She produced her fake driver's license and waited. Mother had a crew of geniuses when it came to creating documentation. No worries there.

"I'll ring the lieutenant for you," he offered, handing back the license.

A lieutenant...she didn't think pencil pushers rose that high in the ranks.

Within seconds, the door to her left swung open with a reluctant groan and grind, and the man who had been behind the window stood before her.

"Wait here," he instructed after she entered. "The lieutenant will be with you momentarily."

He flat-handed a button on the wall, and the door at her back closed with a resounding thunk. Then after handing her a visitor's pass with her name scrawled upon it, he went back to sorting and filing.

She slid the cord attached to the pass over her head, the cardboard square dangled annoyingly between her breasts. There was absolutely nothing of interest to see as she waited, just a long hall straight ahead, ending in a wall with another door. When said door opened, she sucked in a breath of surprise.

There must be some mistake. The man striding toward her couldn't be Tanner Jackson. Dressed in a black t-shirt, camo cargo pants, and rugged lace up boots, he looked ready for a special ops mission, not a day of wrestling with figures and scientific data. Tall and well-muscled, he appeared rock solid, like he belonged in the age of Athena. In fact, he seemed so overwhelmingly masculine, she worried he might not be human. That gave her pause. Had the Reps already established a man on the inside?

Other than Reps, she had nothing against alternate species, including humans. She just liked to know for sure with whom or what she was dealing. Double standard of course, as she had no intentions of letting this man know her Fae status.

His dark brown hair, curiously well beyond regulation length, curled past the nape of his neck, and even darker brown eyes studied her as he drew near. He halted before her, his arms crossed over his broad chest, his stance slightly spread to give maximum stability.

Without a word, he reached for the I.D. dangling from the strap around her neck. The back of his hand grazed across her breasts, and her nipples swelled and grew taut making very noticeable peaks beneath the thin material of her over blouse.

"Miss Goodeve." He nodded. "I'm Tanner Jackson. Everything appears in extremely good order." His lips twitched just short of a smile as he scrutinized the information on her badge and her naughty nipples. "If you will follow me," he suggested, although he remained in place, an immovable hunk of male pulchritude, "we can talk more comfortably in the conference room."

"I had hoped for a tour of the facility," she said, snatching the card from his hand.

His commanding presence made her feel out of control, not an acceptable condition unless she happened to be in his bed. Oh for crying Cassiopeia, this was not the time for randy thoughts and daydreams. Right now she needed her wits about her. She clamped her lips together and returned his unyielding stare, all the while wondering what secrets he knew as she fought the urge to become lost in the dark depths of his eyes.

"I'm afraid your request is out of the question," he said, snapping her back to reality. "We're on level six lockdown. Any higher and our interview would have been cancelled, a true shame as I would have been very sorry to disappoint you."

She doubted he could disappoint a woman in any capacity. "Why the high security?" she asked, following as he turned and headed for the door he'd come through. "Let's start the interview with that question."

He gave a little snort of amusement and escorted her to a comfortable room housing a table, plush chairs, a small fridge and a coffee machine. Not waiting for her, he took to a chair and scrubbed a hand across his face. Only now did she notice the shadowy smudges beneath his eyes. He looked like he needed a good night's sleep. Again her mind strayed to a vivid image of him in bed. It hadn't taken long for her to disregard her vow to swear-off Earth men. Cursing her racing hormones, she took the chair across from him and pulled out her hand-held to record their conversation.

"No taping," he said.

"But…"

"Some areas have voice activated security checkpoints."

With a huff she reached for the recording device intending click it on as she shoved it back inside her purse. He grabbed her wrist and stopped her cold then calmly relieved her of the little contraption, removed the back panel, and flipped out the rechargeable battery. With a knowing look, he deposited the pieces back into her hand.

Calling up her best expression of sarcastic disdain, she dumped everything inside her purse and dug around for a pen and paper. The back of her grocery list would have to do.

He still hadn't answered her first question, but by now she couldn't remember what it had been so she tried another.

"Maybe you could tell me more of what you do here." She had a basic idea but was curious to see what he would reveal.

"How about some coffee?" he asked, rising and heading toward the coffee maker. Again he avoided answering her question. This was going to be a fascinating interview.

"I'd prefer tea," she said, just to be obstinate.

Not missing a beat, he accommodated the request. For a big man he moved easily, just short of graceful, as he went about the mundane chore. How could he stand to work in an office capacity, cruelly forcing his gorgeous body to sit in a chair behind a computer day after day? He looked like he should be on the frontlines saving the world from the disaster she feared they were heading for.

"Straight up or fancy?" he asked.

"Straight up is fine." It didn't really matter as she hated tea and had no intentions of drinking it.

He set the cup before her along with a little plate of cookies. How sweet, now she felt guilty about requesting the tea. After resuming his seat, tasting his coffee, and eating a cookie in two bites, he stared at her like a hopeful child waiting for her to do the same. Left with little choice, she took a nibble of cookie and braved a sip of tea.

"Very good. Thank you." If he noticed her grimace, he didn't let on. He seemed so out of place here, again it crossed her mind the Reps had already infiltrated the NDGC and he might be an agent. The revisited idea made her stomach heave more than the tea. Out of habit, she gave a few sniffs in his direction, all the while ruing the Reps new odor masking abilities. Then she studied his eyes looking for any hint of a nictitating membrane. He held her gaze and smiled innocently. Might as well ask the obvious.

"You don't look like a computer nerd," she bluntly stated. "To be honest you're the last type of guy I expected to find crunching data."

He gave a soft chuckle, apparently not insulted by her candor. The sound melted through her like warm honey. "My usual job is underwater research, construction, and demolition."

"Then you're a Navy Seal type." If he had connections to the government, with their high security

40

clearance program, there would be less chance of him being a Rep.

"Army Ranger," he quickly corrected. He sounded a bit peeved at having been labelled a Seal.

"So why are you hanging out here?

"An unplanned underwater explosion ruptured an eardrum. Now I'm landlocked for a while."

"I thought Seals did the underwater work."

"Rangers know how to swim, too." His voice took on an even harder edge as if she had dared to question his and the Army's abilities to match skills with the Navy toe to toe.

She guessed it sounded like a plausible and remarkably handy scenario for his reason to be here. Or maybe his getting hurt hadn't been an accident. Or maybe he hadn't been hurt at all. He leaned back in his chair and locked his hands behind his head. Frick he was so ruggedly handsome and darn self-assured. Please, please, let him be one of the "good guys".

"Will you be here long? I mean out of commission for very much longer."

He leaned forward, arms now resting on the table. His expression turned pensive. "I can't remember why you're conducting this interview," he said, avoiding her questioning for the third time.

"Oh, well, my sisters and I run an environmental research agency called the Green Goddess, and we thought knowing what you did here might be interesting and of service to us in some capacity."

"You help big business find ways around the rules and regs?" he asked, a dangerous edge now flavoring his words.

"No," she blurted. "On the contrary. We're trying

to stop—We're trying to preserve the environment. It seems in need of all the help it can get."

He kept studying her as if trying to define her true intent. Then he seemed to come to a conclusion. "A good bit of our work is global."

*All the more reason the Reps would want to get their hands on your data and retrieval.*

"Do you enjoy flying?" he asked.

The question nearly brought her out of her chair. Could he be trying to determine if she were Fae?

"What do you mean?" she countered.

"Flying, you know in a plane, a glider, a balloon. There are lots of skydivers around here. I've been thinking of getting in a few jumps while I'm still in the area."

"Yes, well, flying is nice."

Her wingports twitched. This morning, Bliss had massaged the kinks out of her back muscles and done a little passive therapy on her. She could finally materialize and extend her training wings, even levitate a few inches. She had no doubt full-flight would soon be possible, which reminded her, the steel tips on her wings needed sharpening. They'd been due for maintenance prior to her clash with that stinking Rep, Mr. White.

"Can you tell me more about the satellite systems you monitor?" she asked, trying to steer him away from more questions on flying.

Hoping for an answer, but not expecting one, it surprised her when he obliged.

"Our polar orbiting environmental satellites, or POES, carry a suite of instruments for measuring the flux of energetic ions and electrons at the altitude of the satellite. The readings will vary based on solar and geomagnetic activity.

"Space Weather data is collected via the Defense Meteorological Satellite Program spacecraft. The DMSP includes a sun synchronous satellite system, a special sensor topside ionosphere plasma sensor, a special sensor auroral particle spectrometer, and a special sensor magnetometer."

She tossed down her pen and glared across the table at him. He was purposely spewing out information faster than she could write, and what little she had managed to record made no sense to her. All she knew was it sounded important.

"I'll make sure you get a brochure before you leave," he teased.

"Thanks." *Smart ass*. But she had no intentions of letting him off the hook so easily. "Maybe you could describe, in general terms, the basic purpose of these satellites."

"Okay, fair enough. We monitor solar flares, influxes in radiation, and disturbances from the earth's magnetic fields. In other words, anything which might interrupt, misalign, or fry our equipment. The satellites we use these days are designed to be small and light so they're cheaper to launch. On the down side, they have less shielding and less backup programming. Their signal output is higher, but because they're flown closer together, it means any environmental problems will affect them in clusters. In short, they are more vulnerable than the older satellites."

"Wreaking havoc with them sounds an objective relatively easy to attain."

"Yes, if you had the capability of launching orbital

weaponry, or access to our setup here."

"What effect would be caused by putting several, or all of them, out of commission?" She just had to ask, knowing she pushed the boundaries of what he was likely to tell her.

"What does that have to do with your local environmental agency?" he parried.

"Nothing," she smiled. "Just general curiosity." Besides, she knew dang well what would ensue. Communication chaos, or rather the lack of communication thus causing chaos, and a whole lot of panic. Maybe even disruption of the Nation's power grid.

The lieutenant checked the industrial looking watch strapped to his left wrist. "Gotta go," he said, pushing up out of his chair. "Maybe you could come back another time for the tour you wanted."

Had she touched a nerve, or could he really be pressed for time? Gaining her feet, she noted again his engaging height. Admittedly prejudicial, she couldn't help but be attracted to males taller than herself. It appealed to her vulnerable side, a part of her generally well hidden and ignored by the demands of her chosen profession and species.

As she walked beside him toward the door, she felt disappointed at leaving so soon, the blow somewhat cushioned by the thought of seeing the lieutenant again. Next time she'd wear something more seductive.

He halted and grabbed a brochure off a nearby counter. "May I borrow your pen?"

Retrieving the one from the bottom of her purse, she handed it to him. He scribbled something at the bottom of the leaflet, and handed both back to her.

She tucked the items away and offered him a business card. "Don't forget about my tour. Call me—anytime."

*Day or night* shot through her mind, stopping just short of her mouth.

****

Tanner watched her leave. His gaze locked onto the sweet curve of her backside as she moseyed down the hall on those long, long legs. He sighed and fought the urge to adjust the fit of his cargo pants, wondering what she might really be up to. Seemed awfully curious, her showing up here for an interview the same morning they found Ralphie dead.

Ralph Henderson was a nice guy—had been a nice guy. The idea of his being gone took some getting used to. Like most data analysts, Ralph had been a bit on the dorky side, but he could be a lot of fun, too. Of all the ways in the world a body could die, he'd never expected his little buddy to buy it skydiving. It seemed out of character. Another reason making his death so hard to fathom.

Until they had the autopsy report, they wouldn't know for sure. But foul play couldn't be ruled out. Everybody was on high alert, especially the security division. Last week, the computer files housing personnel data had been compromised. The hacker hadn't gained access to the mainframe containing the top secret data storage, or the control data programs which directed the satellites, still it made everyone uneasy.

Ralphie had been good at his job, and replacing him wouldn't be easy. The thought of interviewing candidates made him shudder. He'd rather face a school of barracuda rather than a horde of wannabes.

His thoughts wandered back to Miss Goodeve. She hadn't looked back as she disappeared out the door. But she'd twitched when he'd asked about flying. Maybe she had a fear of heights. Surely she wouldn't know anything about Ralphie's death. He hoped she'd make good on her promise to come back. If she didn't, maybe he'd visit her office. What a looker, tall and willowy, with long black hair he had the urge to get tangled up in.

Of course there didn't seem much point in getting involved with anyone when he might only be here temporarily. He'd never considered himself the love 'em and leave 'em type and didn't plan to start now. On the other hand, his last long term relationship hadn't gone well either. He seemed to attract women who needed to be rescued, then they wanted to conquer their savior, turning into diva's always demanding their own way. To him, a partnership in any capacity should include compromise. Even the toughest guys he knew wanted to be relieved of duty once in a while, wanted to be taken care of as well as needed. Maybe he should junk all previously preconceived ideas, go for broke, and take whatever Miss Goodeve might offer. If indeed she ever did.

He shook his head. Why all the soul-searching? Guess Ralphie's death hit him harder than he thought, shattering the feeling of immortality which went along with the missions and situations an Army Ranger faced in the field. You couldn't dwell on the possibility of death when you worked at the tongue of the ocean with explosives, sharks, and twenty ton rigging. Or when you were night jumping into enemy territory on the other side of the globe.

Again he pictured Solace Goodeve. Solace. He wondered whether she lived up to her name.

Chapter Five

Tanner Jackson turned out to be an intriguing surprise, one Solace certainly wanted to investigate. She decided not to share that part of the interview with her sisters. At least not yet.

Reining in her horse beneath a large cottonwood tree, she waited for Bliss and Portence. Mother had arranged for each of them to have a mount stabled nearby, and they were to meet up this afternoon for a short trail ride. Solace loved horses—Faes loved horses—a good gallop felt one step away from flying. In the olden days, the clans would often go trooping, especially in the summer when the forest felt cool and faerie flowers were in bloom. Riding also burned up wayward energy while offering a place outside the apartment and office where the three of them could speak freely. As her sisters entered the lane up ahead, she trotted over to them and slowed to a walk.

"So what's the scoop over at NOAA?" Port asked, as they ambled along three abreast.

"He was reluctantly accommodating," Solace acknowledged, "didn't divulge much of interest, and left me feeling he knew more than he was telling. Something is going on—they were at level six lockdown."

"You got that right," Bliss said. "Mother called while we were setting up the computers. A man named

Ralph Henderson, a member of their staff, died this very morning. Did Mr. Jackson—"

"It's Lieutenant Jackson," Solace corrected.

"Okay…did Lieutenant Jackson mention anything about this?"

"No. Not a hint. The only unusual topic of conversation came when he asked if I liked to fly."

Bliss and Portence reined to an abrupt halt. She followed suit, and heads together, their horses slow danced in a little circle.

"Leapin' Sundogs." Bliss gasped. "That guy died skydiving."

The very thought of plunging to one's death made Solace sick to her stomach. Could this recent tragedy be why Tanner asked if she liked to fly? A paradox of feelings raced through her. Having wings, such a death seemed impossible and at the same time horrifying. "What a terrible way to go."

"Do you think you could meet up again with your lieutenant and get more specific information?" Port asked. "Get inside his head?"

She'd rather get inside his pants. Tanner Jackson triggered emotions now running wild. And she liked feeling alive again in ways she hadn't experienced since losing Duncan. Just the thought of Tanner sent little flutters chasing one another through her belly—with more substantial tremors forging a lower path. She squirmed in the saddle and tried to remember Port's question.

"What? Oh, yes. I'm supposed to go back for a tour. We didn't set a date, but I gave him our card, and he wrote his cell phone number on the brochure he gave me. I'll call and set something up."

"We better ask Mother to finagle three top priority clearances for us," Port suggested. "That way you might be allowed into restricted areas, and Bliss and I will have them available should we need them on our assignments."

"Good idea," Solace agreed, wishing she hadn't mentioned the phone number. Maybe her sisters hadn't picked up on it.

"So," Bliss probed, "he gave you his personal phone number. Was he cute?"

*Busted.* "Yes," she grinned, "extremely."

She gave the little mare an encouraging kick and hung on tight as her mount leaped forward and galloped down the path, leaving Bliss and Port in the dust. The reprieve would be short lived, but it gave her a few minutes to gather her thoughts while they raced to catch up with her.

****

Solace floated in the hot tub. Port and Bliss, still adjusting to Earth time, had again called it an early night, but she still felt too wound up to sleep.

She glanced down at her body. Thanks to Bliss' special salve and her own innate Fae healing power, her bruises were but a memory, her muscles barely stiff and sore. In her mind, however, the frightful ordeal of facing off with a Rep lingered on—in vivid detail.

She shook her head as if to dislodge the images. With so many planets from which to choose, it seemed a shame the Reptilians had their black little hearts set on conquering Earth. Perhaps somewhere deep in their genetic makeup, the Tuatara remembered this as home too, and for them it was retaliation. Although she fought under Mother's flag and owed the humans nothing, she felt compassion for them.

Comforted by the buoyancy of the water, Solace's thoughts strayed from war tactics to peacetime activities. She reached for her margarita, draining the glass, and as the water played seductively over her body, thoughts of Lieutenant Jackson played through her mind. Gliding one hand across her bare midriff, she ached at the thought of it being his hand caressing her, his fingers exciting her flesh. Could there be something in the earth water that made her so preoccupied with sex?

The phone rang, catapulting her out of her randy fantasy. She grabbed the receiver, glad now she'd placed it on the table beside the tub. Tanner's name flashed across the incoming call indicator.

"Hello, Lieutenant," she answered, heart pounding in her chest. "I was just thinking about you." *Wrong, wrong, wrong,* she should have said something else. At the dead silence, she felt like a silly Saturn Sundrifter.

"Great minds," he said, politely. "What are you doing tomorrow?"

"Why?" she sparred, not willing to admit she had nothing on her agenda.

"I have the day off and wondered if you'd like to go skydiving."

Jerking to attention too quickly, she slid off the hot tub seat and under the water. Grabbing the edge with one hand, she held the phone above water with the other and fought to relocate her bare bottom onto the slippery seat.

"Sounds like fun," she lied.

"Ever been before?"

She'd been flying since she was three months old.

"No, but I'm always open to new experiences." *Like what it would feel like to kiss your gorgeous mouth.*

"We'd have to get an early start. That okay with you?"

"What do you call early?" she questioned, being more of a night creature.

"Pick you up at 0500."

The very idea made her gag. "But couldn't we—" The dial tone hummed in her ear.

She clicked off the phone and set it aside. Oh, terrific. She never looked her best in the morning, could barely think straight. And with the idea of spending tomorrow with her hunky lieutenant teasing around in her brain, the likelihood of getting a good night's sleep seemed slim to none. By five a.m. she'd look like something a Draconian bearcat dragged in. But wouldn't it all be worth it to spend the day with Tanner? A spasm of desire speared straight to her core setting her once more to fantasizing. By Mithras, she needed a good—sliding under the water, she tried to drown out the idea. Surfacing, she blew out a big breath and a bucket load of unfulfilled desire.

At least her mission to see the lieutenant again would be fulfilled, not that she'd had anything to do with making the arrangements. But in truth, it could be a prime opportunity for learning more about the goings on at NOAA. Except she wouldn't be at the building— she'd be at 13,000 feet.

\*\*\*\*

Tucking her blouse into her jeans, Solace slipped into and zipped up the hoodie, dropped down into a chair, and jammed her feet into sturdy boots. Offering bleary-eyed solidarity, Bliss and Portence sat at the dining room table clutching steaming mugs of coffee as they watched her. She glanced out the window. Darkness still reigned, making her feel like she was stumbling through a bad dream.

"I can't believe you're doing this," Bliss mumbled.

"Me neither," Solace admitted. "It reminds me of boot camp."

She'd managed to choke down a piece of toast but couldn't accommodate more. Snagging an apple, she shoved it in a pocket for later and picked up her hat and settled it on her head.

"A cowboy hat for skydiving?" Port quipped.

"I look good in it," she threw back, with a grin. "And with any luck, there'll be more to this day than jumping out of a plane."

"Oh really," Bliss said, coming out of her stupor. "Such as?"

"Nothing in particular, just a little fun."

"I think you have a thing for this Tanner Jackson. And while he may not be the enemy," Port warned, "he could very well be a stumbling block to getting to them. And since you didn't tell him, how does he know where we live? Sounds like he's doing a little investigating of his own."

A good point. Their business card only gave their work address. The buzzer by the door shrieked, saving her from answering.

"Gotta run." Crossing the room, she pressed the intercom button. "Lieutenant Jackson?"

"Roger that," came the answer. He sounded all military and manly, and a weird fluttering erupted in her chest again.

"I'll be right down." She released the button and

grabbed her purse.

"Be careful," Bliss and Port said in unison.

"I will. I'm wearing my personal GPS so you'll know my location if I need help. Don't work too hard," she called over her shoulder, laughing at their sulky expressions. Slamming the door shut, she deflected the heated sensation aimed in her direction.

**\*\*\*\***

Claustrophobia set in with a vengeance, and not just from being inside this tin can the humans called an airplane. It had to do with being strapped into thirty pounds of restrictive clothing and equipment. Solace couldn't move, couldn't breathe. She wanted to rip everything off, activate her wing ports, and leap out of the plane right now before they even reached the jump-site.

All morning she'd sat through the preliminary instruction course, watching Tanner more often than the instructor. No doubt he'd made hundreds of jumps, nothing new there for him. She had a feeling he was here because of Ralph's death, not because of a desire to really go skydiving.

Possessing an eidetic memory, she had everything down pat as to what she should do and when, and since they would be jumping on a static-line, no freefalling, what could possibly go wrong? It sounded easy enough while they were on the ground. But now, as they approached the jump zone, she began to regret going along with this folly. Her heart pounded as if she'd guzzled five cups of high-test latte, an Earth delectable for which she had developed a fond addiction.

"You go first," Tanner hollered over the sound of wind blasting in through the open door. "I'll be right behind you. Don't look so worried," he added, although his gaze held its share of concern. "You'll do fine."

Swallowing her fear, she nodded, and gave the thumbs up sign.

He slapped the top of her helmet making sure it was on tight. She wished her cowboy hat sat on her head instead. She looked much better in that. Guess she'd have to hold onto the hope of surviving to wear it another day.

He touched the tip of her nose as it peeked out from beneath the oversized and horrendously unflattering goggles, and the urge to kiss him streaked through her. But the plethora of equipment they wore would never allow their lips to make contact. The perfect birth control outfit.

Grinning as if harboring the same thoughts, he turned her around.

"It's time," the pilot said, with a nod. "We're over target."

She took a deep breath and crawled out on the strut.

"Go, go, go," the instructor hollered, reaching out and nudging her shoulder.

She let go, and stomach in her mouth floated free. A few seconds later, the static-line jerked her parachute open, and she drifted over the drop zone. With a sigh of relief, she craned her neck and watched Tanner exit. His chute deployed, but only partially. She could see a slit in the canopy as if the seam had come open. His descent came a bit too fast and erratic. Employing the techniques they had just learned, she maneuvered closer then hesitated. If their lines tangled, they would both be in trouble.

The plane tipped its wings, arcing in a big circle to land nearby and meet up with them on the ground. Too late now for the instructor or anybody else to help Tanner. Anybody except for her. Praying to the East, Spirit of the air, she felt the air thicken as she hit the emergency release on the harness, unbuttoned her blouse, and wiggled free of both. Freefalling for a few seconds, she activated her wing ports as well as her scrambler. It didn't render her invisible, she just couldn't be seen. There really was a difference.

Arms at her sides, she rocketed over to Tanner. The now dense air slowed his decent a little, but not enough. He wrestled with his equipment, trying to jettison the deficient main chute so he could deploy the emergency one, but nothing seemed to be working.

Coming up behind him and keeping low to avoid the tangle of ropes, she grabbed hold of his shoulder straps and held tight. Their descent slowed dramatically. Tanner turned his head from side to side as if he were trying to see what was going on, and she fought the pull of gravity on their combined weight.

She had never flown carrying such a weight load before. Cupping her wings, newly returned to working order, she strained with the effort and tried to catch as much air as possible. Maybe she should have gone with battle gear rather than a light model built for high altitude. The ground, coming up fast, had her worried. Then, thank goodness, their speed became manageable. Like a Canada goose coming in for a landing, she tipped the air out of her wings, and when they were close to the ground, she let go and backpedaled away from Tanner.

He hit the ground with a yelp, no forward roll like

they'd been taught. Then he just lay there on the ground not moving. At least he appeared to be breathing.

Glancing around, she searched for her discarded parachute—and more importantly her blouse. There they were. Setting down nearby, she retracted her wings and fetched her clothing—and none too soon. Tanner, on his feet, helmet in hand, began calling her name, searching for her. When he turned away, she disabled the cloaking spell.

"Over here," she yelled, blouse buttoned just in time.

He half-ran half-stumbled in her direction. She sank to the ground, pretending to feel faint. He crouched down beside her.

"Are you all right?" He pushed his goggles up onto his forehead and studied her face. Removing her helmet and untangling her hair from her goggles, he began probing her body as if searching for broken bones. He worked her arms one at a time to see if they functioned, and she felt like a child after crash landing for the first time.

"It was the weirdest thing," he said. "I couldn't find you. It almost seemed as if you had disappeared."

She eased away from him and gained her feet. He seemed to have no problem focusing now as he scrambled up beside her. Why did he keep staring at her?

"You probably had some kind of brain trauma," she suggested, dusting her hands together to dislodge the dirt and pieces of newly mowed grass. "I was so worried about you. What happened to your chute?"

"Good question." His expression hardened, in fact he looked mad as hell. He would make a formidable enemy to face in hand-to-hand combat. "Let's find out," he added, snatching the goggles completely from his head.

In a very sweet and companionable gesture, he took her hand and led her all the way over to his abandoned chute. They stared down at the snarled mess of fabric, risers, and lines. Letting her hand slip away, he began pawing through the yards of material.

"Son of a—Look at those tears. They caused the chute to collapse, sending me into a tailspin." He shook his head and glanced over at her. "It's a miracle I'm alive."

"You must have a guardian angel or something."

"Something." Again, his gaze pinned her in place.

Enough of this pussyfooting around. Neither of them could do their job if they didn't start working together rather than against one another.

"What's really going on?" she dared to ask. "It appears this was done on purpose."

He remained silent. His yummy mouth compressed into a flat no nonsense line.

"I know about Ralph Henderson," she pressed.

She had all his attention now, but he still seemed hesitant to open up to her. She wrestled her new top security I.D. from the back pocket of her too tight jeans, and flipped it open. He slid it from her hand, his fingers grazing her palm. The touch, so quick, so innocent, went deep, making her inhale sharply and wish for more. He studied the I.D., then her, still remaining silent.

Late last night, Mother had rush-delivered three new and improved badges to them, along with a message indicating Lieutenant Jackson's position at

NOAA had nothing to do with an underwater accident. He had been reassigned following an injury while on a mission in Libya. There wasn't anything wrong with his ears, *or to her way of thinking the rest of his body*, which explained why he was able to go up to such a high altitude today and not risk re-injury to said eardrum. He was Black-Op.

Apparently, the United States government had picked up on the rumors of some kind of worldwide unrest. And although unsure of who or what the danger might be, they'd heeded the rumblings and were trying to be proactive. Tanner was assigned here to keep an eye on things at NOAA. And she was here to help—if he would only trust her.

They stared at one another, sizing each other up with new appreciation, new questions, new possibilities. As his gaze drifted over her, he raised a brow, his look going from curious to hungry. She glanced down. In her haste, she'd skipped a button on her blouse and the edges were lopsided. The gap offered a daring glimpse of cleavage created by her new pushup bra.

Still facing her, Tanner leaned in, reached around, and slipped her I.D. back into her jeans pocket. Then he boldly unfastened the first three buttons of her blouse as if to correct the misalignment problem. Abandoning the task half completed, he surprised her by placing his hands on her arms and drawing her close for the kiss she'd been craving.

Crushed up against the wide expanse of his chest, surprise turned to wanting, and she not only allowed him the brash liberty, she kissed him back. Tall and powerful, he made her feel safe—from what she didn't particularly know or at the moment care. Adrenalin, still running high from the sabotaged parachute drop, raced through her body adding to the heady euphoria.

She wanted to drop to the ground and wrap the two of them in the seclusion of yards of colored canopy, wanted to feel the weight of him on top of her, the feel of his hands taking even more liberties. Something about him turned her on fast and hard. Nothing she could put her finger on, but everything she wanted to put her hands on.

His tongue begged for entrance. She parted her lips, encouraging him, teasing back with equal enthusiasm. Suddenly, as if it took great effort, he gave a muffled groan and pulled away, his breath coming deep and fast, matching hers. Had the smoldering encounter thrown him off balance too? His questioning expression said yes.

"You taste good," he said, easing the edges of her blouse together. "Too good," he added, leaving her wondering exactly what that meant.

As he didn't seem intent on re-buttoning her blouse, she brushed his hands aside and saw to it herself. "Well, if the taste test is over," she said, getting a grip, "we need to figure out what the heck happened to your chute."

Suddenly, she felt irritated for giving in so easily to the attraction he kindled. She needed to maintain the upper hand if their interactions were going to be of any help to Mother. And what made him so darn sure she would welcome his advances? What if she had a male friend, or just wasn't interested. How would he know? His presumption led her to believe he rarely got turned down.

Brow furrowed as if coming to his senses, he turned and glanced at the chute. Had their "moment" been so all consuming he'd forgotten he had just nearly been killed, in fact would have been, had she not been with him.

"It's the weirdest thing," he said, stepping around the area, glancing at the ground, before looking up into the sky. "I'm not actually sure what happened. I know the chute fouled and the safety wouldn't deploy. I swear I was spinning out of control, plunging downward at a fatal rate of speed. Then it felt as if someone grabbed the back of my harness, and everything went into slow motion. After I hit the ground, I looked around and couldn't see you anywhere."

"You were in shock," she insisted, trying to steer him away from the fact he couldn't locate her. "Who do you think slashed your canopy?"

"I'm guessing the same pricks who engineered Ralphie's farewell jump. As far as I know, he used the same school. But I didn't tell anyone I planned on coming here today—other than you." He took a step closer. Fire again flashed in his eyes, but this time it spoke of anger, not hunger for another kiss. He reached for her. "Who did you tell?"

Chapter Six

"I didn't tell anyone."

Solace jerked free of Tanner's grip and took a step back. Could he tell she had lied? Her sisters knew all about today's *outing*, but they didn't count. Remembering her new I.D., she stood her ground. "Since I have top priority clearance, maybe I should be the one asking questions."

Confusion replaced his expression of anger, and he opened his mouth to speak then closed it, evidently changing his mind.

The twin-engine plane from which they'd jumped touched down nearby and taxied closer. Tanner didn't even glance at her as the two men inside reached out to help them climb aboard and stow their gear. After they were seated, he remained silent, but she could almost feel the intense gaze he targeted in her direction. As they gained speed and took off, the pilot glanced back over his shoulder, eyeing her as if she'd just sprouted horns.

"You'll want to take a look at the jump footage when we get back, Lieutenant," the instructor hollered, over the grinding engine noise.

Flying rats. In her panic to save Tanner, she'd forgotten their adventure was being videotaped for posterity. This could prove tricky. How would her cloaking device appear on camera, and how could she explain the situation? She spent the entire flight back to the airfield working out different scenarios in her mind. None of them sounded convincing. If worst came to worst, she could contact Mother and beg permission to inform Tanner of their covert operation. Assuming he believed her, it would make things a lot easier if everything came out in the open and they were working together, but it would also be risky, and what about the pilot and instructor? Or maybe Mother could perform one of her mind-delete procedures. The only trouble being, the memories were erased in timeframe blocks, not specific moments. She'd hate for Tanner to forget their first kiss.

****

The instructor slipped the DVD into the machine and hit play.

She held her breath. *Take off, jump, her chute opening, his malfunctioning.* She let out the big breath she'd been holding and sucked in a normal one. Her image appeared as a dark blur, as if something on the disc or the recorder had malfunctioned. It masked her movements and anything she did trying to help, even if her body came between Tanner and the recorder in the belly of the plane. The instructor fiddled with the dials on the DVD player, but fine tuning didn't seem to help. She was off the hook. Enhancement couldn't beat enchantment.

"Too bad," she said, as her heart-rate slowed. "Looks like your recording equipment had a glitch." All three men glared at her. "But it doesn't explain what happened to your chute Tanner," she said, pushing the point and sending her own meaningful glare at the instructor and pilot.

He nodded and took to pacing about the small room. "I'll have it sent over to the Boulder PD. The forensic team can take a look at it. Maybe whoever did this left some DNA. They can also compare my chute to Ralphie's. There could be a connection."

"Great idea." *Yeah, DNA evidence would be really helpful, if you had Reptilian samples in your data base.* "I still want a tour of NOAA," she reminded.

"Regardless of your clearance, I'm guessing such a request won't be allowed for a few days."

"I understand," she capitulated. Arguing with their safety protocol might seem suspicious.

Mind in a whirl, she tried to come up with some other way for them to see one another. "We're hosting a business event Saturday night," she said, in desperation. "I hope you'll come."

Seeing Tanner remained important—and not only because she craved to do so on a personal level. It was necessary to keep the lines of communication open, and she had to get inside the facility. In the future, Mother might need to run a defensive operation from there. Or should it be taken over by the Reps, requiring the Fae Army to storm the facility, nothing would be as valuable as firsthand knowledge.

"The Green Goddess Environmental Agency is giving a get-to-know-you party for several local institutions and corporations," she explained. "Our way of introducing ourselves to the neighborhood, which we're hoping will prove beneficial for all concerned."

He studied her as if deciding whether or not she had some ulterior motive, which of course she did, but they were on the same side, so it wasn't really a lie. She offered him her best smile and tried to channel Bliss' talent for captivating men.

"I'll be there," he finally said.

Her shoulders sagged in relief. "Will you let me know if you find out anything definitive regarding what happened out there today?"

"Oh, sure. And you do the same."

He added the last like a challenge, as if he darn well knew she had been holding something back.

"Of course," she replied. "See you Saturday. I guess you know the address."

He grinned like a little boy caught in a lie. "We have an extensive data base at NOAA. And what we don't have can always be hacked."

Leave, now, she told her body, but her heart wanted to linger, wanted to keep looking at this hunk of man who despite nearly falling to his death a mere few hours ago, now stood calmly before her. He had the constitution of a warrior, and the kind of steel-nerves and brains needed for heroic quick decisions on the field of battle. If he'd been Fae, he'd be perfect.

****

The party, in full swing, boasted a better than good turnout, and their penthouse apartment worked as the perfect venue for their catered affair. The night, clear and lit by the moon, offered just enough breeze to allow them to keep the big sliders open leading to the wraparound balcony. Everyone seemed to be having a good time.

"We pulled it off," Port whispered.

"I didn't think we could," Bliss chimed in, "not with the two days' notice you gave us."

"I couldn't help myself," Solace defended. "Besides, spur of the moment or not, you gotta admit, it's a great idea. There are representatives here from nearly forty green-minded firms." She glanced around. "Have either of you met your primary objectives?"

"Mine's over there." Bliss nodded toward the kitchen. "His name is Nathaniel Winston Calhoun. He works at the Boulder facility housing the Cesium Fountain Atomic clock."

"He's kinda cute," Solace said, "in a geeky kinda way."

"Why is he hiding out in the kitchen?" Port asked.

"He's not hiding," Bliss defended, "he's shy. And I think he's cute, too. Apparently his boss *made* him come, otherwise I'm not sure he would have shown up. But I'm betting there's a red blooded bad-boy lurking behind those horn-rimmed glasses and that tweed sport coat. You know, still waters etc. etc."

As the waiter sailed by with a tray, Solace snagged an hors d'oeuvre. "What's so important about this clock where he works?"

"Well for one thing," Bliss said, "it's used to synchronize telecommunication systems."

"Is that all?" Port put in, looking bored.

"And NASDAQ uses it daily to time-stamp hundreds of billions of dollars in stock trades and financial transactions," Bliss added.

"Well now, this sounds more interesting," Port relented. "Money being the root of all evil. Or in our case, evil looking for money in order to set down roots."

"Have you talked to him, made plans for a tour of his location?" Solace asked.

"I tried." Bliss chuckled. "He wouldn't commit to a date. I brought him a Mai Tai. Thought I'd give him a while for the alcohol to take effect, and try again later."

"Well my guy isn't here yet," Port said, with a huff and a flip of silky white hair.

"You actually sound disappointed." Solace gave Port the once over. "What gives?"

"His dossier seemed vague, but for a human, his photo did appear rather appealing," Port admitted.

"We'd best check the temperature in Hades," Bliss teased. "Are you ready to renege on your sworn oath not to mingle with Humes?"

"Never. And up until now, it's not been much of a challenge," Port insisted. "My contact is stationed in Colorado Springs. Maybe that's why he isn't here. I'll try and reach him on Monday."

"What's he doing down in the Springs?" Bliss asked, as she gave a little smile and a wave to her special Hume. By the end of the night, Solace knew Mr. Nathaniel Winston Calhoun would be putty in her sister's hands.

"His name is Chance McCall," Port said. "He's with the 721$^{st}$ Mission Support Group. They pretty much run Cheyenne Mountain."

"No kidding? I can see why Mother put him on the list."

Solace couldn't help but be impressed. The underground bunker where this guy worked was the most impenetrable command center on Earth. It also served as the Governmental Epicenter should Washington D.C. fall under attack. And with two 25 ton blast doors, it could handle threats ranging from natural disasters and conventional assaults, to nuclear bombs and electromagnetic pulse attacks.

"Maybe that's him," Bliss said, with a nod of her

head.

Solace and Port turned to see who had walked in.

"No. He's mine," Solace said, with a smile. "And Fae or not, he makes my blue blood boil."

Tanner stood just inside the door, surveying the crowd as if he expected something sinister might be afoot. He'd changed his black op's outfit for jeans, a white T-shirt, and a brown leather bomber jacket—all of which clung to his body like they had been molded to fit only him. His hair, slicked back as if he just got out of the shower, had her longing to muss it up but good.

When he spotted her, his shoulders relaxed a bit then he ambled her way.

"Hi," she said, "glad you could make it." Did her voice sound as breathless to him as it did to her? "Lieutenant Jackson, these are my sisters, Bliss and Portence"

Like most people seeing the three of them together for the first time, his eyes widened in surprise, but only slightly, and he didn't utter the usual hackneyed responses they were accustomed to enduring.

"A pleasure, ladies. And please, call me Tanner."

His smile seemed sincere, but the gaze directed their way appeared to be of a more serious nature. In fact, the word intense came to mind. Why did she get the feeling he'd come here for more than socializing. Again she wondered what might be running through his mind, and what his job really consisted of prior to coming to NOAA.

Silence abounded as Port and Bliss checked him out.

"Care to have a peek at our amazing view?" she

offered, rescuing him from further scrutiny.

"Sure."

He fell in step beside her, snagging a microbrewery beer as they passed the counter set up as a beverage station. A margarita sounded good to her, but she'd already had three and needed to keep her cool, which sounded more difficult by the moment as she studied Tanner standing there in a secluded corner of the balcony.

The moonlight cast shadows, sharpening the plains of his cheeks and deepening the penetrating gaze he fixed on her face. What would he look like in bed with those pensive eyes filled with desire? He seemed so big and sturdy, and she wanted to succumb to the shelter his arms could offer. What she'd experienced with the fellow she'd met several weeks ago had simply been sex, somewhat appeasing, but awfully mechanical. She had a feeling with Tanner, it would be different. With him, she'd be able to really let go and fully give herself over to the emotions she felt right now.

He gave a quirky smile. "You look like you're aglow."

Cripes, she forgot the effect full moon rays had on Fae body chemistry and tribal tattoos. She stepped back into the shadows. Tanner set his beer on the rail of the balcony and followed, as if he thought it an invitation. But an invitation to what? Oh, that's what. With the wall at her back, she became pleasantly trapped between the hard bricks and his hard body. He planted one hand on either side of her, at shoulder level, and leaning in took her mouth in a rough kiss that gentled as she kissed him back. Sweet desire and hot need quickly heated to the boiling point, setting her body on a path leading straight to trouble.

He slid both hands up under her halter top, making her glad the style hadn't allowed for wearing a bra. As he cupped her bare breasts, her nipples grew taut, and a moan curled in her throat.

"God you're beautiful," he crooned, against her cheek, his breath warm, his thumbs grazing back and forth across skin already gone beyond tingling to hyperglory.

She eased her hands inside the leather jacket, skimming across his T-shirt, noting the contrast of firm muscle lying just beneath the softness of the fabric. Hips in full contact with hers, she felt the part of him promising an even better time to come. She pressed her hands against his chest, easing him back. His gaze nailed her in place, devoid of question or apology, leaving only raw passion and intention showing in his eyes.

Turning away, she took one of his hands and led him farther down the wrap-around balcony until they came to the sliding glass doors of her bedroom. She eased one open, and they slipped inside, the glimmering moonlight painting the room a magical silver and black. Facing Tanner, she pushed the leather jacket up off his shoulders. It hit the ground with a heavy thud. Then she unbuckled his belt and the top button on his jeans. Leaving him to do the rest, she kicked off her high-heeled sandals, wiggled out of her mini skirt, and untied her halter top.

Down to one single piece of clothing each, they stood face to face. Wearing only his boxers, which did little to disguise what waited underneath, he ran the fingertips of one hand inside the elastic of her red, silk, bikini underwear.

"This is more of an introduction to your company than I expected," he said.

"It's an introduction to me, not the company," she corrected.

"If this is the introduction, I can hardly wait for the finale."

"Me either."

She pushed him onto the bed and climbed onboard. Gathering her hair to one side, she dipped down to capture his mouth with a serious kiss. As he ran his hands across her back and shoulders, her wing ports twitched. Had he felt it? Too bad they couldn't both sprout wings and fly.

Again her ports twitched and tingled beneath his touch. She hesitated but relaxed as he gripped the cheeks of her bottom and pressed her hips closer, making sure they made contact in all the right places. Guess he hadn't noticed anything unusual.

Tongues dancing, they moved together, the two skimpy layers of clothing a tantalizing barrier allowing pleasure, but inhibiting what they really craved. She drew back and smiled down at him. His eyes had darkened beyond their usual deep hypnotic brown. Then as if searching for something, he glanced first at his jeans on the floor, then at her bedside table.

"Maybe we should…" he said.

She gently pressed two fingers across his mouth. "I'm on the pill," she lied. Mating with humans could only result in off-spring with a great deal of scientific intervention. They were good to go.

"And I'm clean," she added. "The workup for high level security clearance went beyond thorough."

"They put me through the same when I joined NOAA. Guess we're good to go."

He grinned, and with a growl twisted her sideways onto her back. Somehow, in one smooth move, he managed to lose his boxers and end up on top of her. Grasping one of her wrists in each of his hands, he urged her arms upward until she could feel the headboard. Nudging her legs apart, he tempted her through the paper-thin layer of silk she still wore.

Kissing and nuzzling her neck, the "torture" continued until she felt ready to lose herself to a place existing only between lovers.

"Not yet," he whispered, as if privy to her frenzied excitement.

Releasing her wrists, he eased onto his side.

"More," she panted, dazed at having been sidetracked from reaching the ultimate physical goal.

"Trust me," he said, peeling the red silk downward to below her knees.

She kicked free of them, and as she lay at his side, he stroked the part of her now revealed. His touch, gentle at first, calmed her heart rate enough to bring her back to where her senses perceived every detail of what he was doing to her. But when he deepened his touch, her world blurred into mindless passion, and she cried out, and rocked against his hand.

Lusting for it all, she tightened her grip on the part of his body pressed hard against her thigh. Channeling her desire into each stroke seemed to fuel his pleasure, and his stuttering gasp foretold the waiting had come to an end. Rising up he covered her body with his, taking her with one deep plunge and full-blown enthusiasm. Knees bent and hips thrusting, she met each downward motion with equal passion. They moved together as if they had been partners in this dance many times before—with memorable success. It was the next best thing to flying.

This is what she wanted, needed. What she thought she might never feel again. With seemingly boundless physical strength, he brought her to the highest peaks of pleasure. His powerful body moving effortlessly as he gave as much as he took—never letting up—as if he could make love all night and never break a sweat.

Time seemed suspended, the world existing only for them. She rode the wave building inside of her, quickly reaching the crest. Cries of delight mingled with groans of pleasure, ending in mutual and multiple gasps of satisfaction as he pressed deep one last time and held onto her.

"Holy—" Still possessing her, he rose up on his forearms and studied her face. His hair no longer slicked back, dipped forward framing a face she could get used to seeing hovering over her on a regular basis.

She sighed and gave a throaty laugh. "Holy, indeed."

His breathing came in ragged gasps as he smiled back, his cheeks ruddy from passion shared. A near perfect male human, he was also her number one contact at NOAA. Had she screwed up such an important relationship by screwing him? Need and desire satiated, other feelings intruded, like guilt for being sidetracked and not putting her job ahead of her pleasures.

"I should get back to the party." The words came out wrong, sounding more dismissive than intended.

His gaze hardened. Without comment he rolled

sideways, breaking the intimate connection. She turned to face him, grazing her hand across the wide expanse of his chest, the smattering of dark hair noticeably crisp beneath her fingertips. She hadn't meant to so brutally kill the moment.

"I'd really rather not," she added, hoping he heard the sincerity in her voice. "You were wonderful, it was wonderful."

He reached out and smoothed her hair back from her face then cupped her under the chin. His gaze turned searching, as if he were trying to discern her trustworthiness or true motivation, and it occurred to her while she was a good warrior, maybe one of the best on Alpha Team, she wasn't really very good at subterfuge. She wanted to confide in him, not hide her feelings, wanted to tell him she didn't want this to be a one night stand.

His glance wavered, and his expression changed from searching to surprised and curious. Without looking, she knew the object of his fascination. He was staring over her shoulder at her particle laser recharger standing against the far wall. She scooted off the bed, blocking his view as she retrieved her skirt and wiggled into it. She couldn't find her top. Snatching up a rumpled coverlet from the floor, she nonchalantly draped it over the equipment. Then as if continuing to straighten the room, she grabbed a pillow which had also found its way to the floor and tossed it at him.

Standing beside the bed, she reached for one of his hands, and urged him to his feet. With not one ounce of self-consciousness, he stood naked before her, his stance relaxed yet not masking the energy stored and waiting for release in his hard muscled form.

"Really, I should get back to our other guests. My sisters will rag me for days for leaving all the entertaining to them."

"Wouldn't want you to get into trouble," he said.

Gathering the fall of hair covering the front of her body, he swept it aside and back over her shoulders. Then he leaned down and kissed her breasts, giving each nipple a quick suckle and nip. "I'm sure they miss you," he said, straightening to his full height. "You're exceptionally good at entertaining."

She glided her hands across his chest, her fingers coming to rest lightly on his shoulders. She could smell his essence and their lovemaking, it mingled into one special scent, different from anything else in the cosmos, and she registered this olfactory byte in the back of her mind, never to be forgotten. With great effort, she fought the wicked desire to go crazy on him a second time, fought to keep focused on the party and the mission.

****

As he headed for home, the taste of her lingered in his mouth. Tanner wanted her again—right now. He hadn't felt this turned on since he couldn't remember when. There was something special about Solace. Something he couldn't define. To be honest, he didn't even want to try, only wanted to do it with her again.

*Slow down*, instinct warned. *You hardly know this woman.* His position at NOAA allowed access to restricted material and restricted areas, he needed to be careful. But she had clearance, right? Still, with the untimely death of Ralphie, and his own mishap all too fresh in his mind, taking anything or anyone for granted could be fatal. Of course dying with her in his arms would be a heck of lot better way to go than a skydiving accident.

## Chapter Seven

What the heck was going on? Tanner still couldn't believe his commander had okayed a no holds barred facility tour for Little Miss Goodeve. Especially after this morning's NORAD incident over at Peterson Air Force Base. Evidently she had the-powers-that-be twisted around her little finger—just like he would be, if he allowed himself.

A smiled eased the tension from his face, and the feeling reached all the way to his heart. He couldn't stop thinking about her, and what they had done. Unexpected and unintentional, hooking up at her party had really ratcheted up the heat. And although three days had passed, he hadn't cooled off yet. Couldn't get her out of his head.

He entered the conference room and set out the orientation material for the department new hire. Of all days for Solace to come here, he also had to get a rooky settled in. Thompson's résumé had been nearly perfect, he could easily step into Ralphie's position, but nobody could replace Ralphie's dry wit and slightly off-center personality. Tanner sure did miss the little Einstein. It still surprised everybody he'd gone skydiving. Surprised nothing, it had been a total shock, and the last thing anyone could imagine Ralphie going for. The guy had turned pale when someone suggested management create a rooftop lunch area.

He checked his watch and wondered what Thompson would be like. His first name, also Tom, said little for the creativity of his parents, but you couldn't blame a guy for that. If he got the newbie started on paperwork, which should keep him busy until noon, it would give him the time he needed to show Solace around. But a full tour? The unusual request had him on red alert; who did she know to pull off such an invitation?

**\*\*\*\***

Here she came, on time, and hotter than ever. Her blue jeans hugged her hips good and tight, and he recalled what her sweet ass looked like naked. Her blouse, prim, white, and long-sleeved, created an image that clashed in his mind with the red spiked heels she sported. Hair pulled back, tortoiseshell glasses in place, she was a six-foot-four bombshell, making him glad he was good at demolition.

Being tall, but thankfully not the skinny emaciated model type, she fit his ideal of the perfect woman. Bony females were not for him, he always felt he might accidently crush them in the throes of making love. He needed someone who could keep up with him in bed. Solace had seemed surprisingly strong, yet gracefully athletic, reminding him of the female warriors of ancient Greece. Amazons, in their most romantic form. On a Special Ops mission to Turkey, he'd visited the town of Samsun. At the Amazon Village Museum, they had a huge iconic statue of a fierce female warrior flanked by buildings shaped like lions. She would have fit right in.

"Good morning, Lieutenant."

"Miss Goodeve," he acknowledged, with a nod.

Best to keep things formal with other staff members around. He wanted to maneuver her into an empty room and kiss the business-like expression off her face as he explored what waited beneath that blouse. "If you will follow me, please." Unable to resist, he leaned in close, muttering for her ears only. "Darlin', you look sexy as all get out today."

"Why should today be any different," she sassed back before rewarding him with a naughty smile.

Leading the way to NOAA's inner sanctum, they passed the boardroom where Thompson sat hunched over a tutorial. Maybe he'd better check in with the newbie. Altering course he entered the room, Solace on his heels.

"How's it going Thompson?"

"Just fine," the big man returned.

"I'm Solace Goodeve." She stepped forward and introduced herself before he had a chance.

Thompson gained his feet to shake hands. Again he found Thompson's size impressive, not unusually tall, but built like a linebacker, one made of brick.

An odd look came over Solace's face. Her eyes narrowed, and he swore she sniffed the air like a woodland creature smelling for wildfire smoke. Thompson made a guttural sound but didn't say anything.

"Well, carry on," Tanner said, ending the awkward silence. "I'll be back to check on you again later."

He took Solace by the elbow and escorted her out of the room. She kept looking over her shoulder, and Thompson just stood there staring after the both of them.

"What was that?" he asked, as they made their way

down the corridor.

"What was what?"

"That. You two looking at one another like a deer and an elephant surprised to find one another in the same valley.

"Nice metaphor, but your testosterone is showing," she said. "Men frequently *look* at me," she added, matter-of-factly.

"Yeah, I bet. But with lust or desire. Not caution and suspicion."

"I don't know what you mean. Maybe he thought he knew me from somewhere. He looked kind of familiar to me."

Although far from satisfied with her response, he let the matter ride.

At the first lab, he pressed the palm of his hand against the security panel on the wall, and the door swooshed opened. Solace seemed very businesslike this morning. If all she wanted was a tour, then that's what she'd get.

"Our Boulder facility employs approximately four-hundred scientists, technicians, and auxiliary personnel," he began, by rote. "This room tracks environmental satellites, which provide data from space to monitor the Earth's coastal waters, relay life-saving emergency beacons, and track tropical storms and hurricanes. The Earth System Research Laboratory (ESRL) constitutes one of the country's most significant concentrations of scientific expertise."

"Great, very nice. Now tell me something I don't know," Solace said. "Since I last saw you, I've read all the material you gave me and studied what's on-line. I even took the Tuesday fifty-cent tour. I need to know what you guys are up to that a foreign entity might be interested in knowing about or disrupting."

He took her by the upper arm and all but dragged her out of the room and down the hallway.

"I mean it, Solace. What's going on? Who do you really work for?"

She opened her mouth then closed it, and those lips he coveted flattened into a line of determination barring words she seemed to be fighting to hold back.

"If you have to ask, I can't tell you," she finally said, her gaze searching his face as if she sought some grand truth, her expression almost one of pain. "I really do need to see everything."

Tanner balled his hands into fists, trying to keep his cool. Accustomed to giving orders, blindly taking them went against the grain. It went against his instincts. It went against his training. What if she were lying? The stuff she was about to see was beyond top secret. It was experimental, and in the wrong hands, it could bring down an entire country.

"Please," she said.

Although unspoken, the words *trust me* seemed to fill the space between them.

"It truly is important," she added.

Tanner stepped in front of her. She didn't blink or flinch, but rather she calmly returned his malevolent glare, the one he'd perfected to scare his worst combat enemies. Her show of toughness turned him on. And friend or enemy, he wanted her—right here, right now. He eased closer, his body pressing hers back against the wall. Recollections of being with her at the party and the stolen kisses on her balcony flooded his mind. "Are you remembering what we shared that night?" he asked.

In answer to his question, a hint of a smile curved those luscious lips. "Business first," she whispered, against his cheek. "I promise it will be worth the wait."

"I intend to see you keep that promise," he said, bumping his hips up against hers.

She didn't respond and left with only anticipation and his imagination, he turned away, wishing he could appear just as cool and detached. Striding onward, he led the way along a series of corridors and down three flights of steps to a blank wall in a storage unit.

Retrieving a keycard from his pocket, he used it to open a cupboard then pressed his palm against the security panel now revealed. The wall to their left slid open with barely a whisper. Relocking the little cabinet, he waved her through then followed. After hand-printing a similar panel inside, the door closed.

****

This was more like it. Maximum security meant maximum importance.

Solace glanced at Tanner and gave a little smile. His cool gaze didn't waver. Okay, so he was peeved at being left out of the loop. She didn't blame him, would in fact feel the same way if the tables were turned. She had practically bullied him into giving her the tour, and his superiors had backed her up, more fuel for his fire of ire. Solace hated being so secretive and borderline bitchy, but if the job called for it, she could play the part.

She wanted to trust Tanner, felt almost a hundred percent sure she could, but rules were rules. The one about business first had been a hard one to keep. She wanted nothing more than to get at him again. His broad-shouldered confident aura made it hard to concentrate. And remembering how he'd made her feel, and what she'd like to do, made her nipples ache.

They reached an elevator, got in, and began the decent. Trying not to panic, she took several slow deep breaths. How far underground were they going? A shiver of unease tensed her shoulders, and a cold remembered darkness seeped through to the bone. Unlike trolls and dwarfs, her ancestral Earth Fae had not done well after being condemned to live deep below the earth's surface. Apparently, a thousand years had not erased the dread from her DNA—speaking of which.

"Did your forensic people find anything interesting on your parachute or Ralph's?" she asked, trying not to think about where they were.

"They picked up matching samples from each one, but didn't get a hit when they ran the DNA through Homeland Security files."

"No prior record, I guess," she said.

He studied her closely. "They aren't even sure the samples are human."

This information told her all she needed to know. "Maybe it became contaminated, tainted somehow."

"Maybe."

The elevator stopped, and the doors swooshed open. Tanner stepped out and led the way.

"We're in the belly of the beast now," he said, ending any further discussion of their previous subject. "There are three labs down here, similar to the ones upstairs, geophysical, earth system research, and space weather prediction. The difference is, down here we don't gather the data—we create it."

That gave her pause.

"This is the Earth System Research Lab." Halting before a huge Plexiglas wall, he didn't seem inclined to go through the door on the left, so she visually scanned the room. It housed several large computers and a myriad of instruments, some familiar some obviously experimental.

"Gaining control over the connection between weather and climate, and understanding the phenomenon between the climate and water, is a top priority. Water is life, and just like land, they aren't making any more of it."

She tried to ask a question, but he'd moved on through another door in the hallway. Hurrying to keep up, she took her place beside him in front of second glass wall identical to the first.

"This is Weather Forecasting, rather a misnomer as we're nearly capable of creating hurricanes, tornados, and earthquakes, not just predicting them."

*If Mother wasn't careful, she'd be out of a job.*

"Will your new man, Thompson, be assigned down here." Gut instinct prompted the questions. Something about that guy struck her as odd. And by the look on Tanner's face, her question struck him the same way.

"Of course not. The employees down here are complete brainiacs. They've all worked here at least five years, and their combined intelligence makes Mensa look like kindergarten. The new guy will be taking over Ralphie's job."

A sadness shadowed his eyes, and he turned away as if his show of compassion might be mistaken for weakness.

"I'm sorry for the loss of your friend. Good ones are hard to find, sometimes even harder to keep." She thought of Duncan, he'd been her best friend, as well as her lover.

Tanner turned back toward her. "As I'm sure you have already figured out, I'm Special Forces, and I lost several buddies while operating in the Middle East. You just live with the danger. You don't expect all of you will come back. But I wasn't prepared for it to happen here, out of the blue with no reason or warning. Ralphie was young, full of optimism. And he lived for his work. Why would anyone want to take him out?"

"Then you're convinced it wasn't an accident." She threw out the obvious, wondering where it might lead.

This time, his gaze tangled with hers, and it seemed to be his turn to weigh and wonder how much he could trust *her*. Sure would help if they could speak freely, pool their knowledge as well as their skills. Wearing her heels, they stood face-to-face, eye-to-eye. He seemed so controlled and self-contained, yet beneath it all, she thought there lived a man who could use comfort as much as she could. In order to help ensure survival, warriors rarely let down their guard. But eventually, stoicism burdened the soul, and it threatened to damage the inner child they all carried around.

"What I think doesn't matter. What I can prove is what counts." His words were wrapped in determination and laid at her feet like a gauntlet. He definitely wasn't going to give up on finding out the truth behind his friend's death. A reassuring quality, because sooner or later, with any luck, they'd be partnering-up to track down the responsible party.

"We're on the same team you know." It sounded so meager a statement, but the best she had to offer at this time.

"I get that," he countered. "I'm just not sure what position you're playing."

"Just like you, I play whatever position I'm told to play."

She slipped her arm through the crook of his. He gave a snort of resignation and escorted her to the third and final bay of windows.

Stepping away from him, Solace stood up close to the glass. Intent on their work, none of the scientists bothered to glance up. This area, by far the largest, offered corridors leading off in four directions, the purpose of whatever might be housed beyond shielded from prying eyes.

"Upstairs," he explained, "this comparable department monitors solar activity 24/7. Down here they're close to creating it and can already redirect natural sun eruptions. In the wrong hands, the effects would be disastrous."

"So this is the Space Monitoring Station," she said, her mind reeling with scenarios as to how the Reps might plan an attack on NOAA with the hopes of getting their hands on this stuff. If they even knew it existed.

"You've done your homework," he agreed with a nod.

Turning, he led her through one more door. Without windows, the large room remained dimly lit by only two wall lights. Alarm bells went off in her brain. Why would he take her to what looked like a storage/break-room? There were vending machines to the left, a hot plate on a counter, and a few lumpy looking beds along the far wall indicating some of the scientists down here pulled all-nighters.

Just about to demand an answer as to what they were doing in here, Tanner began unbuttoning her blouse, and the hungry look in his eyes removed any doubt as to the answer to her unspoken question. She stepped back. His arms fell to his sides, his expression slipping from surprised to disappointment.

Adjusting her glasses, she peered at him over the tortoiseshell rims and struck a provocative stance. Holding his gaze, she slowly, one by one, slipped free the combs holding her hair in a chignon. Somewhere, she'd read Earth men had fantasies about wayward librarians—reading opened one to so many vistas. Shaking her hair loose, she'd show him naughty, and then some. Glasses and combs set aside, she finished unbuttoning her blouse.

At the sight of her hot pink bra, he growled, grabbed the waistband of her jeans, and yanked her up against his body. Arms around his neck, she flattened her thinly covered breasts against him, and he captured her mouth with his. The kisses he returned with equal hunger and urgency made her dizzy. She wanted him, all of him, right now, this very minute.

Backing her up against the counter, he nudged his right leg between hers, and she rode his thigh, the rough contact and demanding pressure turning her on more and more. Framing her face with his hands, he paused for a second, before his mouth again took hers, swallowing her moan as he tasted her fully.

Trailing his fingers across her shoulders and down her arms, he nuzzled her neck, and she gasped in a much needed breath. When he wedged one hand down the front of her jeans, the snap popped open, and the zipper split and lowered of its own accord giving him clear access to her. She clung to his shoulders, writhing against him, wanting to get at him in kind, as his fingers worked their magic.

Somewhere a floorboard creaked, momentarily snagging her attention. What if someone came down the hall? What if they came in? They hadn't locked the door. They hadn't—oh Goddess. As he deepened his touch, she didn't give a rip if the entire NOAA staff assembled alphabetically in front of them. There was no way she could stop now.

Gathering her wits about her, she managed to undo his jeans. He'd gone commando and spilled out big, hard, and full of promise. Wrapping her fingers around him, she gave a quick squeeze then stroked and petted, teasing the tip with her thumb.

The hand he'd had down her pants stilled, and with a groan, he pressed closer, nipping at her neck, alternating tiny kisses and little nibbles. A shockwave of heat stormed through her. Shifting his hand from her pants to her bra, he unhooked the front closure and cupped one breast. He kissed her there, tasting the already aching flesh, teasing nipples hard as ripe cherries. She pushed the breast he favored against his mouth, wanting to give him more, wanting to give him everything he desired. His strength and power seemed to flow into her, blending with her inner being, affecting her in a way she hadn't felt the first time they were together. This seemed different, this felt special.

"Get inside me, now," she breathed against his cheek.

He slid his hands from her body, and with one sweeping motion sent coffee filters, stir stix, and paper cups flying off the counter. Then he pushed her jeans down over her hips. They fell to her ankles, and she stepped out of them, along with her red heels. Hands around her waist, he lifted her up and set her on the edge of the Formica. The blast of cold went straight through her silk underwear to the cheeks of her butt. She gasped, but the feeling dissolved away as Tanner snagged her shoes off the floor, and one by one, slipped them back onto her feet. She felt like Cinderella, a very wayward, very sexy Cinderella. He ran his hands up her legs from ankle to knees, eased her thighs apart, and stood between them, the strip of hot pink covering her crotch creating no barrier as he slid it to one side and filled her body and her needs.

Head back, she moaned loud and clear, and wrapping her legs around him, used the leverage to get full penetration as he led her beyond all bounds of self-control. With one hand at the small of her back, he held her upright. With the other he cupped one breast, roughing her nipple with his thumb, coaxing more sensations from her. Kissing her right ear, he nipped at the lobe and nuzzled his face in her hair, all the time never breaking stride, never breaking the rhythm sending her higher and higher.

"You're driving me crazy, babe," he gritted between breaths as he continued to quicken the pace.

She tightened her legs around him, red heels meshing at the small of his back. "Then mission accomplished," she cried, arching against him.

The dark room burst with colors. He wrapped her in a crushing hug, diving to maximum depth, once, twice, his groan of satisfaction echoing around hers. Time and space faded away as she floated free, feeling only hot release ripping through her from the inside out. Head bowed against his shoulder, hands tightly gripping the edge of the counter, she rode the wave pulsing and twisting through her body.

Going limp and barely remaining upright, she opened her eyes. Tanner smiled and kissed her, this time ever so gently. There was no denying it, being with Tanner constituted more than just scratching the itch. She had feelings for him—at the moment, very deep and very satisfying ones.

****

Thompson finished all the forms in record time. He'd reviewed copies of them at Rep headquarters the previous evening and knew exactly what to put down. His human boss, Lieutenant Jackson, didn't seem suspicious, but his brief encounter with Miss Goodeve had nearly turned his eyes red. He'd studied recently arrived pictures of her. She was a Fae Warrior—the one who killed Mr. White. The humans were no problem, they never would be, but the freaking Fae were another story all together. Thank goodness he took all his medications without fail. She hadn't smelled him. It would have caused quite a scene. One which he was not prepared to deal with. He worried again he'd made a mistake, shouldn't have been coaxed into doing this. He supposed in the end it would make little difference.

NOAA was a Reptilian target. They would expect him to report finding a Fae Warrior snooping around. He took several deep breaths in and out to calm his nerves. He mustn't overreact. Nothing to get excited about. Just notify Mr. Smith. It would look funny if he didn't. Everything would be okay.

Chapter Eight

By Mithras, she'd done it again.

Solace stepped out of the shower. Good thing she'd gotten home before her sisters. When she hit the apartment, she reeked of sex. They would have busted her in a heartbeat. After a thorough scrubbing and a few sprays of Crystal Cosmos No. 5, her secret should be safe.

In truth, she really didn't mind the goodhearted teasing their knowing might generate. What a joy it was being with family again. Last evening, since her wingports were fully functional, the three of them had gone on a midnight flight, soaring above the clouds and dive-bombing one another.

Like children, they'd laughed until it hurt, playing hide and seek, and their favorite childhood game *hawk*—an airborne version of chicken. Sometimes they forgot they were full grown and here on a serious mission.

And in that respect, things were moving along too slowly for her liking. Bliss expected to meet up with her clock-geek soon, but Portence had yet to connect with her male counterpart at Cheyenne Mountain. Portence had little patience when it came to men, especially humans. This poor guy was already in trouble and didn't even know it.

Lieutenant Jackson spelled troubled too, but for

other reasons. He made Solace lose control and at the same time feel whole again. A feeling she thought she had lost forever. But she didn't want this. It complicated her life and messed with her head. Both bad situations for doing her job and staying alive.

At least today hadn't been all play and no work, so she needn't feel guilty on that score. Seeing the underground experimental facility firsthand marked a major accomplishment. The Reps must never find out about it, they would definitely rank it at the top of their takeover *to-do-list*.

For his own safety, she longed to tell Tanner everything, but it wasn't her call to make. Still, she needed a logical reason to keep seeing him, other than the obvious. Asking for another tour would be redundant, but he liked the out of doors, maybe they could go hiking. She loved the forest and being outside too. How about a picnic? If he went for such a *girlie* idea, it would be a sure sign he wanted to please her.

Putting the thought aside for a moment, she grabbed up the most recent bundle of Alpha Team Updates, opened the sliding glass door, and sprawled across a lounge chair out on the balcony. First she checked the Rep facial recognition photos. Mother did her best to keep them up to date on what the Reps in each area looked like in human form. Being underground Intel, she wondered how Mother managed to pull off such a coup. Probably best not to ask.

Angling one particular ATU photo toward the sunlight, she squinted at the picture. This guy looked familiar. Sitting bolt upright, she nearly tipped out of her chaise lounge. The grainy rendering made identification a little iffy, but she swore it looked like

Thompson, the man she'd just met at NOAA. The friggin' Reps were already inside.

****

Solace reached downtown Boulder in record time, parked, and silently opened the door to the Green Goddess office. "Gotcha," she said, leaping inside.

Bliss had been reading a mystery on her handheld while Portence worked on painting her nails. They both jumped and shot her looks of surprise, then annoyance.

"I see business is booming." She grabbed a soda from their little fridge and flopped down into a chair. "It's hotter than reentry outside."

"The weather here is totally unpredictable," Bliss agreed, "I'm never sure what to wear."

"Such a dilemma for Miss Manners," Portence jibed. "I'm sticking with black, regardless."

"I think we need to contact Mother," Solace interjected, gaining their complete attention.

"Holy Hector, what for?" The pale expression on Bliss's face said it all. Calling Mother, although not unheard of, must never be taken lightly.

Solace nodded at the jumble of papers and photos on the nearby table. "I'm sure there's a Rep working at NOAA. Met him just this morning. I don't see there's much choice but to get permission to tell Tanner. They're working side by side, sharing coffee and "war" stories. Before long, a slip of the lip or worse could happen."

"Especially since you'd rather put those lips to better use," Portence threw in.

Solace smiled. "That's beside the point. I just had a tour of the underground labs. They're doing experimental work which the Reps would love to get

93

their claws on."

"Sounds like we don't have a choice," Bliss agreed.

Gaining their feet, the three sisters huddled in a circle, joined hands, bowed their heads, and chanted. Ten seconds later the phone rang.

Solace picked up, putting it on speaker.

"Hello my darlings, I assume this is of vital importance."

Mother's good humor took them by surprise. Solace threw a questioning look at her sisters. They shrugged and glanced at one another in mutual confusion. Then a muffled male voice in the background caught their attention, and all three smiled. Mercury must be there, Mother's favorite "messenger boy". He often brought more than good tidings.

"My idea to call," Solace said, fessing up in case there were repercussions, "and you're on speaker phone, with Bliss and Portence. I need permission to inform Lieutenant Jackson about what's going on."

"About what's going on, is a bit vague, Solace. Exactly what do you have in mind?" Mother's voice snapped back to normal, authoritative and a bit scary.

"I'm sure a new employee at NOAA is a Rep." That pretty much said it all.

"Do you trust Lieutenant Jackson? Besides in bed, I mean."

Good grief, was nothing sacred? "I think he's stable enough to hear the truth. He's an Army Ranger, has top clearance, and has been reluctant to confide in me, which would warrant he can keep a secret or two."

Dead silence followed. For a moment she thought they had lost the connection. "Thompson is a Rep, but he's working for us. Counter espionage, double agents, and all that rot, we're playing the game, too."

"Would have been nice to know," Solace said.

"Well we still aren't completely sure where his allegiance lies, and I don't want to spook him. For a Rep, he's rather a nervous type. I was going to give you a heads up soon. We just aren't sure how much we can trust Thompson."

"So what do I tell Tanner?"

"Keep the information general, and in small doses, only what's necessary regarding who you are and what we are up against. Don't tell him about Thompson, yet, if you can avoid it. I'm afraid he might unconsciously blow the Rep's cover."

Solace's shoulders slumped in both relief and defeat. She had permission to let Tanner in on the game, but not warning him about Thompson didn't sit well with her.

"And," Mother added, "for now, no one else. If you don't think he will keep it to himself then don't do it. If he betrays us, you know the consequences."

As the ramifications careened through her mind, she realized her faith in Tanner would be the determining factor in how much she revealed. She might be taking on a situation which could easily spiral out of control.

"Thank you, Mother," she managed to say as calmly as possible.

"Anything else?"

Portence leaned closer to the phone. "My contact at Cheyenne Mountain has yet to respond to my multiple requests for meeting with him. What the heck is up with that—I mean, I became concerned this could be a problem, ma'am."

"Yes, I'm aware he's not available just now," Mother acknowledged. "That area is deemed secure at this time, so I'm not overly worried, nor should you be. Concentrate on the problems at hand, and on keeping your cover secure by running the business."

Portence made a face. Solace knew her sister hated feigning work and being stuck doing nonsense paper pushing. She and Bliss were both champing at the bit to get some real action.

"He'll be worth waiting for," Mother added, with a chuckle.

Well that sounded a bit cryptic. Then the muffled male voice again filtered in from the background.

"Stay safe, Mother out."

They heard a riff of feminine laughter before the connection went dead, and all three of them burst out laughing as well.

"Nice to know Mother also likes getting a little once in a while," Portence said. "But what's this nonsense about this guy I have to babysit being worth the wait. I'm not interested in Humes, no way, no how."

"Guess you'll just have to wait and see," Bliss teased. "Meanwhile there's a stack of filing to be done. And orders are orders."

Portence threw a manila folder at Bliss' head then turned to Solace. "Why the sad face sis. You got the go ahead."

"I know. But it's a case of being careful what you ask for. I thought I'd feel relieved, but I'm more anxious now than ever, and knowing Tanner is breaking bread every day with a Rep isn't easing my mind. Besides, explaining stuff like this to non-Faes is always a bit risky. They either think you're crazy, or they freak out and can't live with the secrets."

She prayed Tanner wouldn't fall into either category. If he rejected not only the idea, but her, it would be a wound to the mission as well as her heart. Guess she'd find out tomorrow.

Chapter Nine

The next day at lunchtime, Tanner dropped off another batch of study material for Thompson. He liked the big son-of-a-gun, although the guy seemed awfully quiet, but then quiet wasn't necessarily a bad trait. And he looked like he could wrestle a bear and not break a sweat. Good man to have at your back.

"I'm leaving early today, so I'll see you in the morning," he called, to the newbie. "If you have questions we can go over them tomorrow."

Since the weather remained warm, Tanner had agreed to take the afternoon off and meet Solace for a picnic. And what man didn't just love a picnic? Of course he'd be willing to endure almost anything to see her again. They were going to hike some lesser known trails he'd discovered in the foothills west of Boulder, so at least part of the day sounded enjoyable.

Thirty minutes later, he swung the big 4x4 pickup into a parking space at the reservoir where they were to meet. He couldn't help but wonder how this day might end. Starving for food as well as for more time alone with Solace, he hoped she brought more than tea sandwiches and lemonade. Maybe he should have stopped off for some fast food on the way. Reaching under the seat, he brought out a pint bottle of whiskey and took a swig. It helped kill the pain. Not in his head or ears, they were just fine, he'd fibbed to her about that, the fake injury being a cover story as to why he'd been assigned to NOAA. No one knew he was Special Ops, or that he was busted up from years of using his body as a weapon. Libya had not only given him new wounds but had reinjured old ones.

He didn't want to complain to HQ, afraid they'd assign him to desk duty for the rest of his life, and he didn't want to start taking pain pills. So a nip now and then did the trick. The doctors said he'd just have to learn to live with the pain. A lot of guys had ended up a lot worse, or hadn't made it at all. A good reminder he was lucky to be alive and still have most of his body parts in working order, hurting or not. With not much in his life to focus on, sometimes he let the pain get too him, let it become a focal point instead of a sideline.

He glanced up and stowed the bottle as Solace's little blue hybrid car screeched around the corner. The woman drove like a bat out of hell, and how in the heck did she get her long lean body into such a tiny vehicle anyway? She popped the trunk, rolled to a stop, and got out of the car—resembling a ballet dancer emerging from a shiny blue gift box. Today, her hair was in one thick braid. She flipped it over one shoulder, gathered her belongings, and with sunhat in place, slammed the trunk closed.

Exiting the truck, he nestled his pistol into the holster he wore. He had a license to carry, and when wandering woods occasioned by mountain lions, bears, and rattlesnakes, it didn't hurt to be armed. He leaned against the hood of the truck and watched her cross the parking lot. What a vision. Picnic basket swinging to and fro, she sauntered his way. The warm breeze plastered the gauzy skirt closer to her body, highlighting her curves, and the tall hiking boots managed to look sturdy and sexy at the same time. The frilly top under her jean jacket dipped low enough to show bits and pieces of her runic tattoos.

The body art she sported fascinated him, but for some reason he hadn't asked about them. Although she never made an attempt to hide the markings, instinct warned they were personal, almost tribal, and not the usual tramp-stamps and whimsical stuff most women came up with. In his business, other than combat scars, distinguishing marks including tattoos were frowned upon and could be dangerous when used for identification by the enemy.

"Hi, sailor. Buy a lady a drink."

He gave a snort of laughter. She came up with some of the darnedest phrases, almost like she came from some other time and place. The other day, she'd actually said bees knees, yet she showed signs of also being into the latest music and street fashions. Maybe she happened to be one of those people with an "old soul", or whatever the New Ager's were spouting these days. Regardless, he liked her off-beat personality.

"Sailor? I told you, I'm Army," he quipped, hoping she would take it as the joke it was meant to be. "Here, let me help you with that." He reached for the picnic basket, but she held back, another blatant example of her independent streak.

Resisting the urge to take her hand, he chuckled and led the way along the edge of the woods to the trail he'd found. After about a half hour of scrambling over the rock strewn uphill trail, they came to a clearing with a small pond—croaking frogs and all.

Although neither of them appeared to need a break,

the place couldn't be more idyllic, too perfect to pass up. He stretched out under a tree. She alighted on a nearby boulder, setting the basket at her side. Hugging her knees close, she leaned back, her face turned upward as if to absorb the dappled sunlight as it slipped between the leafy branches of the tree and up under the brim of her hat.

Her pose, and the filtered lighting, made her appear almost fragile, which he knew couldn't be further from the truth. For her size and stature, she packed an unusual amount of strength and energy. He wished now he'd brought along his camera. He'd left it home because some people found picture taking invasive and inhibiting, and he wanted this day to be one of total calm and leisure, the antithesis of their skydiving debacle.

After a moment, which he wished had gone on a bit longer, she sat up and smiled. But her eyes appeared downright serious.

About to ask what might be troubling her, he held back as a movement behind her caught his attention. A large pond lizard had crawled up on the rock she sat upon. At the risk of being called a sexist, he suspected like most females she harbored an innate fear of frogs, snakes, and other scaly things. Giving her a heads up seemed the right thing to do.

"How do you feel about reptiles?" he asked, keeping his voice calm.

Solace sat bolt upright. Her eyes widened in surprise then narrowed with suspicion. "What do you mean?"

From the expression she wore, he figured she didn't like them. "Don't be alarmed, but there's a rather large, scaly, one behind you."

Solace flung herself to the ground, knocking over the picnic basket while retrieving the weirdest looking pistol he'd ever seen. Then executing a few evasive maneuvers, she ended up in a one-knee combat position, gun in hand.

He leapt to his feet as well, his Jericho 941at the ready.

When Solace sprang upright, they stood back to back, and he searched the perimeter with no idea who or what the target might be.

"What's the matter?" he asked over his shoulder, wondering what in blue blazes had set her off. "What the hell's going on?"

\*\*\*\*

Heart racing, pulse pounding, Solace scoped out the area where she'd been sitting. Then she noticed the big bug-eyed creature bobbing up and down on the rock she'd vacated. Guess she might have overreacted a tad.

"Stand down." She uttered, still in military mode. "I'm sorry, I thought—"

Tanner turned to face her. "You thought what?" His expression held a combination of disbelief and anger. "You got some kind of vendetta against lizards?"

"More than you can imagine, which is why we need to talk. Sit down."

"Uh-oh," he muttered. "Nothing good ever follows the words *we need to talk.*"

She clicked the safety on and slipped her particle laser back into the picnic basket. Then smoothing down her skirt and plucking a few leaves from her hair, she waited for him to comply. He seemed reluctant to holster the Israeli pistol he favored. Then as if coming to a hard won decision, he did so and sat on a fallen log, giving her his undivided attention, his face grim, his eyes questioning. Guess it was now or never to bring Tanner up to date as to exactly what was going on right under his nose.

"I'm Fae," she began.

"I thought your name was Solace." Now he appeared more confused than angry.

"Not like Faye Dunaway or Fay Wray. Fae as in faerie-like."

He didn't speak, just furrowed his brow and squinted up at her.

"You know, faeries, and pixies, and elves oh my."

"You've got to be kidding."

"A Fae Warrior to be exact." She added the last in hopes the combatant association would appeal to him.

"I knew you were too good to be true. Beautiful, sexy, intelligent—and you're a whack job."

There it was. She didn't blame him. But she must convince him, had to get him on their side. They needed him as an ally, and heaven help them and him if he became an enemy.

"You don't believe in anything supernatural or extraterrestrial?" she asked, taking a different tact.

"I didn't say that," he countered. "There are more things in heaven and earth, yada yada, but come on, faeries?"

At least he seemed willing to listen, and since for most people, seeing was believing, she decided to try a visual.

With an innocent little smile, she conjured a set of wings. Not a sweet ethereal pair to accessorize her outfit, but a full blown class-A combat set. They were light as feathers, but tougher than steel, and the ends were rimmed with talons hard as diamonds—and sparkly too. She always thought that was a nice touch for battle dress. Then the physical body enhancements which accompanied the transformation flashed through her. Her eyes focused a bit more keenly, a fiery element adding to their green hue, and her ears grew pointy. The conversion also pumped up her muscles, and she stretched a bit taller in preparation for battle.

Mouth agape, Tanner reared back. With an imperceptible leap, she shot straight up off the ground, gained treetop level and hovered, doing a few pirouettes just to show off.

He lurched to his feet, appeared stunned, yet somehow still not convinced. Calling to the East, spirit of the air, she gave a few flaps of her wings, sending a tsunami of wind rushing through the trees. Limbs bent, leaves dashed about, and the loose dirt whirled around in an impressive dust-devil. After the wind passed, she struck a flower-faerie pose and floated downward, landing without a sound or a ripple of the tall grass.

Tanner held his ground, his hand resting on the butt of his automatic weapon.

All her senses were in hyper-mode. Cripes, she hoped he didn't intend to shoot her. She considered beclouding, but thought it might panic him all the more. Flash-moving to his side, she placed one hand on his forearm until he relaxed his hand and moved it away from his firearm.

He stepped back, his gaze sweeping her from head to foot. "Damn, woman. What the hell just happened?" Not waiting for an answer, he took several more paces away from her. Then he stood there, his hands fisted, not moving as if to let what he'd just witnessed settle like the dust drifting around them. Finally, he ventured closer to stand before her. She stood tall and silent, fearing to move or somehow scare him away. Tentatively, he reached out and flicked a finger at one of the talons on her wings, and a slight smile fought to capture his mouth.

"If what you're telling me is true, I should probably be running for the hills right now. Because believe me, I'm totally freaked out. But I'm also turned on, and wanting you all the more. I..." He ran a hand across his face as if to clear his mind. "You're the warrior-woman of my dreams." He studied her face then grabbed and kissed her. Definitely not the reaction she had anticipated. "You better tell me the whole story before I lose control all together."

He stroked her wings, this time gently, palm open. She dematerialized them before she lost control, too. Reaching for his hand, she sank down to the ground beneath the tree, and urged him to join her. He slowly complied.

"It's a long story," she began, trying to calm her senses. Tanner's kiss had affected her more drastically then the flood of neuro-stimulators accompanying the combat wings.

"I got nothin' but time," he reassured.

"Okay. Let's start with, do you believe me now about being a Fae Warrior."

"Yes, No, I don't know. I should, after what I just saw. But I'm having trouble wrapping my mind around the idea. It hasn't sunk in yet."

"Remember your skydiving incident?"

"Yes, what's that got to do with—my chute never

recovered, never caught any air did it?"

"No, it didn't. I saved you by deploying wings."

"But it didn't show up on the video. Don't tell me you can turn invisible, too."

"Not exactly. It's more of a cloaking devise, obfuscating or beclouding we call it. We aren't invisible, you just can't see us, there's a difference."

"If you say so." His eyes darkened, and his expression became dead serious. "What's this all about then? Why are you here? And I guess by here I mean not only in Boulder, but on Earth. Or are you from Earth? Who else knows about you? Man I sound like a babbling idiot. And don't give me the old if I tell you, I'll have to kill you, b.s."

She almost laughed, but the truth of what he'd just said quickly sobered her. "Originally we were from Earth, but now we live elsewhere. And I hope I don't have to kill you, but you have to understand I'm taking an awfully big risk telling you any of this."

He sat a little straighter, and his expression turned to a cocky *you could try.* If he thought she had become a threat, would duty demand he kill her too? Would he? Could he?

"So who tampered with the chute?" he finally asked.

"The same people who killed Ralphie."

"Ralphie." His glance slid sideways, but not before she caught the sadness in his eyes. His unspoken compassion said a lot about his character, and what it said she liked.

"And who is that?" he demanded, flashes of anger replacing sorrow.

"What did your forensics team reveal," she hedged.

"I told you, it was weird. The DNA on my chute and Ralphie's matched, but the samples were listed as contaminated because they didn't meet all human parameters. The CSU joked it might be Bigfoot. They also mentioned something about reptiles." He glanced over at the rock where the lizard basked in the sun. "For the last time, dammit, what's this all about? Give."

"They're kinda like lizards."

"Who are?"

"My enemy. Your enemy. They want the earth."

"I'm supposed to believe some scaly little prehistoric throwback is going to conquer the world."

"Yes. But they aren't little."

"So what, they're like alligators. Haven't seen any of those around lately," he scoffed.

"Bigger. And they can look human when they want to. And they like to eat Fae Warriors."

This news seemed to give him pause. Maybe he still felt some connection to her, some need to protect her. She really liked Tanner. In moments when she gave-in to daydreams, she hoped to continue their relationship. But her mission came first, and if it meant giving him up, she'd just have to deal with it.

"Okay, say I believe you. Exactly who are you with?"

Here came the questions. The wheels were really turning now. And the questions indicated he thought there might be some validity to what she'd told him, always a good sign.

"I'm with Fae Warriors Alpha Sector."

"Does the Pentagon know about all this? Maybe you're a lizard. Why haven't I heard about anything from Army HQ?"

"No doubt you will. A few people in your government are aware of our presence, and the Reptiles know we're here, too. Our Commander is only disseminating info on a need to know basis. We didn't realize the enemy had become so well entrenched in such strategic areas."

"You mean NOAA."

"Yes. Which I suspect is why you've been stationed there."

"I knew something majorly important was going on, my office skills suck. So tell me more about these flying salamanders."

"We call them Reps, short for Reptiles. They aren't lizards or salamanders, and thank Jupiter, they can't fly."

As if filled with nervous energy, he scrambled to his feet and paced back and forth. Then stopping, he stared down at her, his expression indicating he wrestled with doubts and the cracked reality her story created in his mind.

"Don't you believe in sentient lifeforms other than humans?" she asked.

"I guess I never doubted there were other beings in the Universe. I just never imagined them being giant faeries and big scaly swamp things."

Giant faeries? How off-putting. I mean she'd seen giants, and generally speaking they weren't a pretty sight.

"So, were you sleeping with me only to gain intel?" He threw the question at her like a well-aimed rock, and it hurt almost as much. Her mind registered surprise, but in her heart she felt sadness. By implication he doubted her and what they'd shared. But then why wouldn't he?

"My assignment included general surveillance, observation of your security set up, and my impression of you being a candidate to join us. Sleeping with you was my call."

"And a darn good one," he finally said. A crooked grin eased across his face, brightening her melancholy, giving her hope they might salvage the newfound relationship they shared.

"Tell me more about these…reptiles." He shook his head. "I can't believe I just said that. Why are they here," he added, once again joining her beneath the tree. "Seems like there's plenty of other planets in the Universe. What's so special about Earth?"

Ever the soldier. Even though he might not truly believe her story about the Reps, if there was the slightest possibility they truly constituted a threat, he wanted to learn all he could about this new enemy.

Leaning sideways, she snagged the handle of the picnic basket and dragged it closer. Settling back against a log, she retrieved two beers from the wicker hamper and handed one to him. In perfect timing, they both twisted off the tops and downed a healthy swallow. She should have brought a canteen of margaritas.

"Part of why they're here," she began, "is retribution. They were exiled from Earth too, a long time ago, even before we left. Another reason why they're here is because humans, or Humes, are pretty easy to conquer."

"That's bull. We have the best military in the world."

"True. But not the best one in the Multiverse. If

Reps arrive here in great enough numbers, you won't be able to stop them. They're bred for killing, and outclass you in brute strength, which means they will eventually outclass you in fire power."

Their enemy had an extensive history, one of wreaking havoc in isolated pockets around the Multiverse. Sometimes they lent muscle behind the scenes, inciting civil wars, or they helped setup dictatorships, even fueling religious conflicts. Other times they just stomped around overtly, crushing and destroying things for no particular reason.

"So then what—you're here to help even the score?"

"Something like that."

He slapped the heel of his hand against his forehead, just making the connection. "Are your sisters faerie warriors too?"

"*Fae* Warriors. And yes of course."

"How many troops do you have here?"

"Can't tell you that."

"Hey, wait a minute. Are there male Fae Warriors too?"

"Yes."

"They must be something to see in action."

"Quite."

"You got a special one flapping his wings just for you."

He sounded jealous. She liked that.

"Had, is the operative word," she said.

"You broke up huh? Being in the military is hard on relationships."

"No. He died."

"Oh, sorry. The military will do that to you, too. In

battle?"

"Yes."

"An honorable way to go."

"Dead is dead," she countered. "Posthumous medals only weigh down a heart already drowning in sorrow. And accolades don't salve the wounds."

He reached for her hand, cradling it in his two strong ones. "I know. I never lost a girlfriend to combat, but I have lost good buddies. Guys I shared a comb with, guys I loved like brothers. You never forget, and there's always the burden of why them not me."

She studied his face. A haunted quality infused his expression, darkening his visage. He really did know how she felt. Another reason she liked him, wanted to be with him. Another reason she needed to back-peddle and get a grip. Sex was one thing, falling for this guy another. There were hard times coming, dangerous times. Protecting her heart needed to be a priority, too.

It sounded good on paper.

\*\*\*\*

Smith wandered about his office as he listened to Thompson report in.

"At least she didn't make me as a Reptile. That's good news, right?"

"Yes, of course. Keep us informed." Smith hung up the phone thinking it really wasn't good news at all.

If that Fae operative kept sniffing around NOAA, it wouldn't take her long to discover they had a man inside. Not much he could do about it now. Changing course would be out of the question, and with Thompson in place, the next phase of the operation would begin soon.

Trying to catch a decent breath, he pulled at the collar of his soft linen shirt and loosened his tie. Maybe it was just nerves. Waiting had never been his strong suit, and they hadn't brought him a woman in nearly two weeks. Apparently, the disappearance of so many female humans had drawn undue attention. But something had to give. He felt a rampage coming on, which would draw unimaginable attention.

He plucked the handkerchief from his breast pocket and blotted the sweat from his forehead. At least in Hume form he had the luxury of fine clothes, and damn he loved driving that Mercedes SLS—he could never fit his real body into one of those. Just like the women, the cars here were too small for his species.

Flipping through the papers on his desk, he reread the latest orders from Head Quarters. Their weaponry hadn't been updated to include particle lasers. It irked him they were always a step behind the Faes. On the plus side, they had procured a drone from Peterson Air Force Base. He doubted information regarding the theft would make the local or national news. After all, how could the U.S. Government claim the theft of an item they weren't supposed to be experimenting with in populated areas?

Although small, the Condor drone would be large enough to do some useful damage. But learning to manually control the weapon with a customized computer program would be crucial, not an easy task. A Hume, up to speed on operating the wicked little device would do nicely, willing or unwilling. Maybe they wouldn't even need the thing. But by-the-devil, having the drone in their arsenal felt reassuring.

He leaned over, shut down his computer, and

punched the intercom button on his desk module.

"Yes, Mr. Smith."

"I've decided to take the day off, Veronica. I'll check messages later."

"Yes, sir. See you in the morning, sir."

He fished the car keys from his pants pocket and headed for the office door which bypassed his secretary and the waiting area. Too bad Veronica didn't appeal to him. She would be a convenient little snack. But then he'd have to advertise and interview for a new secretary. It sounded a poor tradeoff.

Chapter Ten

Ninety-eight, ninety-nine, one hundred. Tanner grimaced with pain and levered up off the floor. Enough push-ups.

Rising before sunup this morning, he'd already done one hundred sit-ups, ran five miles, and swam twenty laps. Pain, like liquid fire, ran through his barely healed shoulder, and his leg came in at a close second as far as throbbing, but he'd toughed it out, no reaching for the bottle anymore.

Since his "talk" with Solace, his mind and body felt hyped up, he couldn't sit still, couldn't focus. And every time he tried, he started to question his sanity. How could Solace be some kind of...of what? An extra-terrestrial, an interstellar traveler, a mythological being come to life. He favored the latter. Adding the childhood fantasy twist to the equation helped to lessen the shock, making it seem like something remembered, rather than new. Yet, even while witnessing her display yesterday, it had been hard to comprehend. And today it seemed impossible to swallow. What she'd revealed changed things, he guessed for her too.

After her revelation, and in between lengthy contemplative silences, they had talked for a long while. When it got dark, they parted ways, the day not ending as he'd planned or imagined. Yet ironically, he felt closer to her.

But right now, trying to think things through logically didn't seem to be working at all. Being a man of action, he saw things in black and white. No matter how dangerous, he'd always followed orders—no questions asked. But whether sanctioned or not, this turn-of-events with Solace left nothing *but* questions, and the few answers he could come up with disturbed him greatly. When a man followed the rules, he expected the Universe to do the same.

Oh sure, he'd known men who had flown in space or had dived as deep as the tongue-of-the-ocean. He'd heard their stories. "Stuff" existed—up there, down there, and out there. Things defying explanation. So why couldn't he accept this at face value? Maybe because now it was personal. He'd made love to Solace, felt something special for her.

At best, relationships were tricky, demanding and deserving time and consideration. None had worked out for him in the past, and there were times he thought human females were so hard to understand they just *might* be some kind of alien species.

He wanted to get past this. Solace had made him think about growing roots. Of course, at the time, he hadn't known who and what she was. Which brought him back around to the most outlandish part of the situation. The total freak out—major turn on issue. Holy crap, he'd had his dick inside an alien—and he'd liked it—a lot.

****

Solace squinted open her eyes, took note of the glaring sun, and pulled the covers over her head. When she'd gotten home last night, her sisters had already gone to bed, but she'd barely gotten any sleep. And when she had, her dreams were filled with visions of Tanner running away from her, his face contorted in horror.

It shouldn't matter, but it did. How easily things had slipped beyond sex to caring. Hopefully he would come around and accept her as Fae. Having been brought up in the Multiverse with multi-species, she tended to forget what an attitude adjustment it took for some beings to accept the concept. Guess time would tell where he stood on the matter. If nothing else, regardless of how he felt about her, they needed his help inside NOAA. Being a soldier of the highest caliber, he wouldn't fail them there.

The door to her room squeaked open, and before she could throw back the covers and defend herself, two assailants hit the bed.

"Well, how did it go?" Bliss asked, bouncing up and down on one side of the bed.

"We're waiting," Port prodded, sitting calmly on the other side, jostling about due to the transfer of motion from Bliss.

Solace scooted up to a sitting position. "I'm not sure. For better or for worse, I think it's going to take some time before it sinks in and he comes to any rational conclusion."

"I'm not sure rationale is going to play a part in this," Port said.

"I had to give a demo to convince him. And he figured out what happened when we went sky diving. It didn't go down exactly how I planned."

"Did you mention Thompson?" Bliss asked.

"No. I didn't want to throw that at him, too. You know, one hurdle at a time. Besides I don't want Tanner taking Thompson out if we can use him. But I told him about the Reps in general, with a quick mention about their propensity for evil and their plans for invasion. He didn't say much. Contrariwise, he didn't go screaming into the woods."

*It was just a dream. Just her worst nightmare as far as interpersonal relationships.*

"When do you see him again?" Bliss, asked.

"Tomorrow. We agreed to a little time apart, and then to meet for lunch."

"You like him don't you," Portence said matter-of-fact, no scolding or teasing.

"Yes," Solace admitted. "More than I thought I could like anyone since losing Duncan." Hearing the declaration out loud took her by surprise. The words, now cast into the Multiverse, would either leap along with joy and a life of their own, or come back to haunt her and bite her in the ass. She wanted the first scenario so badly, she willingly risked the second.

"It's dangerous getting involved with humans," Portence warned. "But I have a feeling you'll win him over. When it comes to men, regardless of species, they're usually willing to believe just about anything if it means getting into your pants."

"Good grief, Port," Bliss said, "could you make it sound any less romantic? True love can conquer all."

"Sorry to wound your sensibilities, baby sister," Portence apologized, although she didn't sound sorry. "Just because you believe in fantasies, doesn't mean Tanner will." The last words were barely out of her mouth when a pillow hit her in the head.

"One of us has to believe in the passion of the spirit as well as the desires of the body," Bliss fired back, searching around for another pillow to throw. "And, by the way, I didn't get my tour of the fountain clock because they're working on a new improved model, but I did get a brief one-on-one with my Hume. With those thick eye-glasses and mild manners, he reminds me of Clark Kent. I'm still betting there's a superman behind the bowtie."

"Uh oh," Solace put in. "She's still hung up on comic book heroes and Japanese Anime adventures like when we were kidlettes."

"Shows what you know," Bliss defended. "Cosplay and Comic-Con are all the rage. Even graphic novels are coming into their own, and action hero movies have never gone out of style."

"Okay," Solace said, with a laugh. "Don't get your wings in a twist. Spill the goods on Clark Kent."

"I told you, his name is Nathaniel, and I dream of mussing up that perfect haircut. I found out he not only works with the atomic clock in Boulder, but coordinates the DGPS coming out of Pueblo, collating and uploading the info to the NDGPS." Bliss beamed a smile their way, knowing full well they didn't know what she was talking about. "What's the matter, a little behind on Mother's current need to know info?"

"Cut the double talk and explain it to us," Port said. "It might begin to make up for all the hours I spent trying to teach you your time tables before we got separated."

"Ya right. I still can't do math. That's definitely not one of my talents."

To be honest, none of them were good with numbers. Splitting the check at lunch the other day had required a calculator. But they were each imbued with special gifts beyond the usual Fae talents. Solace honored the air, and her ability to control the element had helped save Tanner while parachuting. Portence enjoyed playing with fire and had on occasion been known to whip up fork lightning. And Bliss, sweet Bliss, could communicate with and sooth the savage beast in all species and animals—except for Reps unfortunately.

Bliss cleared her throat, and like a child about to give a recitation, sat up straighter. "DGPS means differential global positioning system. Add the N, makes it National. The systems are much more accurate than the GPS in our cell phones and in our cars. Even the Coast Guard uses it at sea, and it guides river and air traffic. It can correct accuracy from fifty feet to a mind blowing five inches."

"Destruction of that setup would have global consequences," Solace said, cocking her head in contemplation.

"Couple it with a Rep-made solar flare," Port added, "and the power grids would be knocked out—leaving no cell phone service to worry about, or energy to pump water."

Bliss nodded. "Things would go from chaos to civil war in a nanosecond when food supplies ran out. And throw in the takeover of Cheyenne Mountain, leaving the U. S. Government with no safe place from which to operate, and the scenario is complete. The Reps could put in their own regime unchallenged."

Solace had to admit, it was quite the impressive battle plan. NOAA, the fountain clock, Cheyenne Mountain, it was a flippin' takeover trifecta. "Port," she asked, "any word yet from your Hume in Colorado

Springs?"

"No," came the answer followed by a huff. "Nary a word. I think Mother is doing this on purpose. She knows I'm the least patient of the three of us."

Solace couldn't argue with her there. But although she lacked patience, Portence came in first as far as being a diehard, from her tenacity on missions to her *old ways or no ways* personal code. And although they all valued their independence, Port had definitely gotten the wanderlust gene.

"Mother's always sneaking in life-lessons when you aren't looking," Port said. "Or running some kind of trickery to amuse herself. Did she do the same to you guys when we were separated?"

"I'll say," Bliss agreed, twirling a lock of red hair. "One time she told me I was going to a training camp with lots of sea views. I ended up saturation-diving in an undersea laboratory on Aqueous II. There's barely a scrap of land there, and the promised sea view came from the bottom up."

"She pulled the same scam on me," Solace admitted, and laughed. "She must have been rotating us around to the same places, but at different times. Too bad we didn't know. We could have left messages for one another and beat her at her own game."

"Oh yeah, that'll be the day when we pull anything over on Mother." Even Portence wisely bowed to Mother Nature's position of power and expertise. Being a little wild and crazy didn't mean they were stupid.

"Speaking of Mother," Bliss inserted. "This morning's message indicated things are really heating up. The Reps are in several areas of strategic importance, not just here but across the country.

Something is about to go down, but no one knows for sure where the fireworks will start or when. We have to stop them. We mustn't allow an all-out war." Her mouth tightened into a frown.

War would take the greatest emotional toll on Bliss. The warrior toughness she turned toward the world shielded a profound gentleness, a characteristic much less evolved in either Solace or Portence. She supposed Bliss's ability to relate to animals demanded a more transcendent personality.

Portence could pull off pragmatic, and Solace fell somewhere in the middle. She always felt in the middle, guess because she *was* in the middle. She had black hair in the middle of unexpected white and stunning red, and she hadn't been coddled like Bliss the younger, nor listened to like Portence the elder. She was just there, in the middle.

She didn't mean to complain, that's just the way things were. And now with all of them together again, she knew Port and Bliss would be there for her, no matter what. Just like she would be for them. It wasn't such a bad deal to be flanked by youth on one side and experience on the other.

When it came to sex, however, she laid claim to the title of most energetic—no more being in the middle on that one. But it took more than just good looks and a rockin' body to inspire her. She had to have some kind of connection, like she'd had with Duncan, like she felt she might be building with Tanner.

His being a Hume presented a few problems. Here on Earth their dissimilar timetable in aging couldn't be ignored, guess there wasn't much she could do about that. She really wanted to make this work, was willing to do whatever it took to make it happen. Only two things seemed to stand in the way of her happy little plan for them to be together, two things she couldn't control—losing him to the whims of war, and the possibility he couldn't accept her as Fae. She'd know at least one of them tomorrow.

As they each sat lost in thought, Solace studied her two sisters. Being together again had a profound effect upon her. While they were apart, she thought she had conquered the loneliness, had learned to live with the heartache, but it had all been an act, a mechanism of preservation, and to be free of such a shackle felt exhilarating—the thought of it returning frightening.

"Whatever happens, whatever is to come, we must always stay together. Promise me sisters mine."

At her words, Port and Bliss scooted closer. Tears glistened in their eyes, and she knew without asking they'd been thinking similar thoughts. Hands joined, their tribal tattoos softly glowing, they closed their eyes, and heads back, chanted the prayer of unity.

Chapter Eleven

Yesterday had seemed like a week or a month, not a mere twenty-four hours. Tanner had almost called Solace last night, but in the end had decided the agreed upon time apart would be important for both of them. Besides, yesterday he'd received orders to appear at Fort Carson this morning, and that had been occupying his mind as well. Located a few hours drive south of Boulder, he left early today, just as the sun hauled itself up and over the eastern plains.

He missed most of the commuter traffic on I-25, but despite the beautiful weather, instinct told him the reason for his being summoned wasn't going to be a good one, and his dark mood soon offset the bright day.

Ever since his last overseas mission, he'd been haunted by the possibility of being permanently reassigned to a desk job. No more Special Ops for him. They were correct, of course, but the truth cut deep. No matter how hard he trained, he would never be the physical specimen he used to be. His injuries were permanent and severe, and the chain of the coveted twelve man team left no room for a weak link. If one man failed, it could mean death for all of them. He understood. He just didn't like the idea.

He'd had a lot of good missions though. Was proud of the job he'd done, and the men with whom he'd served. Only the last deployment, which left his body damaged and too many of his friends dead, made him wish he'd done things differently. But the clarity of hindsight didn't help now. Besides, sabotage never left room for proper planning. Their jump in Libya had been doomed from the beginning, with things in Tripoli quickly going from bad to worse.

They never found out who the informer had been. And any Intel coming out of D.C. had been confused, one answer contradicting the other. When he let it, which happened to be most of the time, the need to make someone pay for his losing five men still ate at him. Trying not to allow this to be one of the times, Tanner cleared his mind as he sat in his C.O.'s office waiting to hear his fate.

When General Harker entered the room, Tanner scrambled to his feet.

"At ease," the man barked, returning his salute. "Have a seat Jackson. I won't mince words. You're a credit to the Rangers, and one of my best men. You're also smart enough to realize you're here for reassignment."

"Yes, sir." Refusing to show any weakness or disappointment, Tanner had nearly shouted out the reply as if he were a raw boot camp recruit.

"Don't take it so hard, son," the General said, seeing though his bravado. "You might be surprised when you hear what the Army has in store for you. As of now, it isn't being offered to anyone else, Ranger or otherwise."

\*\*\*\*

Solace arrived first at the restaurant, keeping her part of the promise to meet here for a late lunch. She liked *Carelli's*. They had great Italian food, and she could get a veggie meal without inhibiting Tanner's choices. He had the aura of a meat eater. Not a problem really, just not where she was coming from. And they served beer as well as wine. She liked beer, finding its earthy quality appealing.

The booth in the back looked like a good choice, offering privacy for their conversation. She wondered how he'd taken the news. Apparently, the United States Military Complex had finally seen the light, and they were taking matters seriously. Their top secret meeting with Mother had no doubt been the catalyst. Wish she could have been a privy to that presentation. Even in Earthly form, Mother could be one heck of a shock jock without half trying.

The light in the restaurant brightened momentarily when the front door opened, and Tanner sauntered in. Every time she saw him, she got a fluttery feeling in the pit of her stomach. You'd think the feeling would wear off after a while, but it hadn't yet. He spotted her, and crossed the room with a nonchalance belying the power and alertness she knew waited just below the surface.

Decked out in his leather bomber jacket and the usual t-shirt and jeans, he smiled as if he knew a secret before he planted himself in the seat across from her. Calmly lounging there, arms crossed over his chest, she guessed the ball was in her court.

"How did your trip to Fort Carson go?"

"Very enlightening."

"In a good way?"

"Yes."

She smiled too.

"You knew all about it didn't you," he accused. "A heads up would have been nice."

"I only found out this morning. Did you accept the inter-planetary training position?"

He nodded, not seeming very talkative.

"I'm glad," she added. "We need men like you on our team."

"What about you, Solace. What do you need?"

The question came as a surprise. She needed *him*, but couldn't bring herself to say so. Their relationship seemed to be changing on a daily basis, sometimes backsliding, sometimes going too fast. Their feelings were new, and the situation they faced so serious. Besides, since her *big reveal*, he hadn't seemed as attracted to her. She should give him an honorable way out. "I don't need anything. But what I want is for us to remain friends."

"Friends? I thought we were way more than that. Or has the time we've spent together been just a ploy, part of your orders to garner my cooperation."

"I've yet to prostitute myself for *the cause*," she snapped, not appreciating his comment. "And I thought we'd already covered this subject." But on second thought, she guessed in a way she had lied to him, at least by omission as to who and what she was. And she had a feeling honesty meant a lot to him, and maybe not just in a professional capacity. Maybe he'd been deceived before in both wartime and where matters of the heart were concerned.

"What I feel for you is real," she reassured.

"And what exactly is that?"

"I…" How do you put something so ethereal and fragile into words? And would it be a mistake to do so? Either way she didn't intend to discuss it right now. "We need to talk about Thompson," she said, abruptly changing the subject. Now definitely onboard, he had a right to know.

He came to attention, all business now, his gaze narrowing as he studied her face. "What about him."

"He's a Rep."

His eyes widened in surprise, and he leaned forward ever so slightly. That certainly seemed to have gotten his mind off their relationship situation.

"What. No way. How do you know?"

"I just do. And it's been confirmed."

Although when she thought about it, she wondered why Thompson had shown absolutely no reaction when meeting her the other day. Not one sign he recognized her as Fae. And she hadn't picked up on him either. Were the Reps getting better at hiding their emotions just as they excelled at hiding their hideous forms and odious smell?

Tanner shook his head as if in disbelief. "But we went to a Rockies game, drank beer, ate hot dogs," he said. "He seems like a regular guy."

"Don't beat yourself up over it. It's one of their greatest strengths. They fit in. And soon they'll have enough men here to execute their plans for taking over."

"It makes sense the Reps would plant a man at NOAA."

She nodded in agreement. "It will definitely be one of their tactical targets. And then there's the Think Tank you've got going on in the basement. I'm not sure that they know about that, and we need to keep it that way."

The memory of what they'd done while touring the basement broke her train of thought, quickening her breath. The heated expression in Tanner's eyes, and his cocky smile indicated the same thoughts were stirring his body as well.

"Maybe we should take another look down there," he suggested, the smile broadening.

Their waitress strolled over before Solace could answer. The girl gave Tanner her undivided attention, and when he ordered spaghetti and meatballs, she acted as if he'd spouted Shakespeare or something equally as fascinating.

"Cheese ravioli for me," Solace put in.

"Be right back," the perky blonde said, her gaze never leaving Tanner's face. She scribbled their orders on her pad, then turned and sashayed toward the kitchen.

"What about the Think Tank," Tanner repeated, getting them back on track.

"If they find out about it, they'll either take it over, forcing the employees to do their bidding, or they'll destroy it and the people working there."

"A grim scenario at best."

"Indeed."

"It's so hard to imagine this is really happening. I mean I'm accustomed to going in guns blazing in defined war zones with known enemies. Right now, everything seems status quo, relatively peaceful."

"Except for a rash of missing prostitutes, and the two other women found mutilated."

"I read about those poor women in the paper. You think the Reps had something to do with that?"

"I know they did."

With a groan of comprehension, Tanner flung himself back against the seat, his expression one of emotional pain. "And they killed Ralphie, and tried to get me too."

"Yes," she confirmed. "They like to keep busy."

Tanner closed his eyes for a moment as if the reality of it had finally hit home, and as if he wanted to erase the disturbing images and information from his mind. Then he opened his eyes and his expression hardened. "So how do we take him down?"

"Thompson? We don't. We just watch him. He was recently recruited on our side. Unless he shows signs of double-crossing us, we leave him alone. If we take him out, they'll just cancel the mission and focus on another objective. We need to capture their soldiers, and hopefully one of their higher-ups."

"So the logic is to stop whatever they're planning in mid-strike, not prevent it from happening?"

"Yes. It's the only way to draw them out."

"Dangerous proposition." He smiled now as if the thought seemed exciting rather than off-putting.

"I know." She smiled back. Finally, another man to match her penchant for adventure and risk taking. "We need to beef up security and put together a plan so we'll be ready for them, and the employees will remain safe."

The waitress returned with their food, dropping the plate of ravioli in front of Solace like a hot brick before ceremoniously setting Tanner's spaghetti before him. "Careful, handsome," she warned. "It's hot."

Solace wasn't sure if their waitress meant the food or her body as the girl struck a provocative pose less than a foot away from their table. Tanner just smiled and winked. The girl blushed, and with a flip of her hair, left them alone.

Solace burst out laughing. "My stars," she gasped,

"does this happen often?"

"Everywhere I go," he said, with a weary theatrical sigh.

She supposed it probably did. He was ruggedly handsome, and so big and capable looking, emanating some kind of *knight in shining armor* vibe. A twinge of jealousy gave her pause, silencing any snappy reply.

"Never did much care for blondes," he added. "Black-haired vixens are more my type."

Head bent, she concentrated on her food, hiding a secret smile.

"When we're done eating," Tanner suggested, "we should go back to my place and talk strategy."

She couldn't think of anything she'd enjoy more, but again duty called.

"Sounds good, but we'll need to make a stop or two on the way. I got clearance for both of us to visit the Boulder PD and the city morgue. We've been asked to take part in solving the recent mutilation deaths of local females. That will have to come first."

Chapter Twelve

The head of the Boulder PD turned out to be surprisingly co-operative. And why not? Another mutilated body had turned up just this morning. They had a serial killer on their hands, committing heinous crimes in their fair city, and not one clue as to who the perpetrator might be. But Mother wouldn't have finagled getting Tanner and herself involved if a Rep wasn't thought to be responsible. They just needed to find out which one. For some reason, Solace didn't think Thompson filled the bill, but they couldn't afford to overlook any possibility.

Sharing their known info with the PD would be disastrous, if in fact they even believed her, so instead Solace collected copies of the crime reports for each victim. After a few phone calls, she also obtained Crime Scene Unit samples so they could run tests in the impromptu lab Mother had set up adjoining the girl's fake office.

"We have plenty of *Mr. White's* blood and DNA on file," she said to Tanner as they left police headquarters. "Some of the women died before I took him out, so I guess we should keep him in the mix. Maybe more than one Rep gets his jollies this way. And we have the DNA from both parachutes. Didn't Thompson have to take a physical of some sort for employment?"

"Yes, of course. But if he's a Rep, like you suspect, he obviously managed to fake the blood work. But I can get some DNA."

"I wouldn't recommend ripping hair out of his head."

"No," Tanner agreed, with a snort of laughter. "I'll grab his coffee mug from work."

"It's a start. Maybe we'll know more after we visit the morgue."

\*\*\*\*

They had both seen their share of death on the battlefield, but brutality out of context, surrounded by the so called civilized world, came as a shock. And now the body count was up to six women.

The first two victims were single working women, both in their late twenties-early thirties. Body number one had been released to the family and had been cremated. After the second death, the police feared a serial killer might be on the loose, and all subsequent bodies were being held pending the open investigation.

The next four were prostitutes, three bodies showing major decomposition as it took longer for anyone to notice they were missing and care enough to call it in. But number four, today's unlucky working girl left in a park, got discovered right away. The Rep was getting sloppy or bold.

They read the ME's report then scrutinized the women lined up for their viewing.

"Dear Lord," Tanner murmured.

Solace pulled on the required latex gloves and closely examined the most recent victim. There were bruises on the woman's arms and legs. None on her throat which ruled out strangulation as the cause of death. The woman's eyes were wide open, her features contorted in pain. Blood loss had been extensive, leaving her skin as white as the salt fields of Darrius III. But it was the condition of the lower half of the woman's body, which made Solace wish for hot sun and clean fresh air. The woman hadn't just been sexually assaulted, she had been torn apart. Her pelvic bones were crushed, there were gouges in her abdomen made from the inside out, and the vaginal area had been barbarically ripped apart."

"Are they all like this?" she asked.

The ME nodded. "I've worked here twenty years, and this is the most gruesome act of human butchery I've ever seen."

*Because a human hadn't caused it.* Even if Mother hadn't confirmed it, she knew in her soul, it had been the Reps.

"There doesn't seem to be anything obvious connecting the victims," she murmured, scanning the police reports.

"Only the terrible way they died," Tanner gritted, jaws clenched.

While they were there, they also picked up the ME's report on Ralph Henderson. She handed it to Tanner, allowing him to read it first. As he scanned the report, he shook his head as if in sorrow. But when he glanced up at her, hot anger showed in his eyes—not sadness.

"He was dead before he fell from the plane. Most of the bruising and the broken bones were postmortem. Poor little guy. I guess they killed him just so we would hire Thompson."

"I'm sorry," she said, placing a hand on his arm.

"If he had to die, I'm glad they did it before they took him up in the plane."

She murmured in agreement then glanced through the police report including both Ralph's death and Tanner's so called mishap.

"It says here," she noted, "although it wasn't tossed, his apartment showed signs of a struggle, which fits in with the ME's findings. They interviewed everyone working at the flight/jump school, and apparently the plane from which he fell was private. It left from their runway but never returned. The flight school figured they landed someplace else, and since they found Ralph over one hundred miles away, it took a while to connect the incident to the small airport. I'm guessing they rigged the chute to try and mask the real cause of death. And the tail numbers were faked so the police were left with little else to go on."

"But what about my chute?"

"The airport didn't report any mischief or break-ins around that time, but one of their new employees failed to show up for work the day after we went flying. He never even came back for his paycheck. Sounds like the darn Reps had a man working there, too. Which is why the DNA on both chutes matches, and why it will never be found in a human database. Staying there after killing Ralph, and taking a crack at you, seems more like dumb luck rather than careful planning. And when you didn't die, sounds like he went to ground."

Determined to rid the earth of these monsters, and knowing they had their job cut out for them, she and Tanner left the building.

**** 

When they reached Tanner's, the place took her by

surprise. He'd rented a house, not an apartment. Old and Victorian in style, it stood far enough from Pearl Street Mall to be quiet, yet close enough to walk to the shops and restaurants should the urge strike.

The décor, however, came off as strictly male. Leather couches and easy chairs huddled football fashion before the fireplace and the huge flat screen TV hanging over the mantel.

The works of art were another story though, and quite stunning. All black and white photographs, blown up and framed with simple stark ebony wood. The desert scenes were almost other-worldly which greatly appealed to her. Several shots contained animals, the usual dogs and cats appearing sad and abandoned, and then more exotic creatures such as wolves, snow leopards, and bears.

"You took these?" she asked, running her hand along a frame housing an image of a particularly large wild goat.

"Yes," he admitted. A hint of pride flavored his voice as he shed his leather jacket and tossed it over the back of a chair. "Part of what I enjoy about visiting foreign lands is discovering their indigenous species."

His attraction to the unusual gave her hope. Did he think of her as a foreign species to be photographed and studied? He still hadn't brought up the fact of her being Fae, yet it didn't feel like a big Barathion Oliphant in the room.

"Besides," he added, "since photography is part of my intelligence training, it naturally followed."

"They're wonderful."

"Thank you. It's one of my few pleasures....up until now. How about a beer?" he quickly offered, heading into what she assumed was the kitchen. "I know you like them so I stocked up." Now, a hint of sheepishness crept into his voice as if he'd been caught enjoying fantasies of her visiting his home—and here she was.

She couldn't help but be flattered, and amused. "Sure, that'd be great." As she waited, she stood by a kitchen window gazing out at the backyard. What was she doing here? She should be making contingency plans for protecting NOAA, or tracking down the local Rep serial killer. And lately, Port and Bliss had been giving her grief for not being around enough and not helping with the undercover company façade. At least she had a batch of new info for the Mother board.

As she watched, a rabbit hopped across the yard, the scene so idyllic it was hard to believe they were likely heading for, if not all out war, at least a frightfully big skirmish.

War...something not to be taken lightly. The sorrow left by war had no name, but she carried it with her always. She needed Tanner, needed to be needed, needed to be desired and made to feel beautiful. It helped to offset the ugliness in this world and in so many others. Still, those were selfish thoughts—the wishes of a woman, not the edicts of a warrior.

Tanner drew closer to stand at her back, the heat from his body a welcome comfort. Like molten metal drawn to an irresistible lodestone, she leaned back, not meaning to, yet unable to stop. He encircled her with his arms, a cold frosty bottle in each hand. "Here's your beer," he said softly, nuzzling the nape of her neck.

The tension drained from her body, and she laid her head back against his shoulder. Based on the unmistakable bulge in his pants making contact with her backside, there was little doubt where this would be heading—if she let it.

He pressed the bottles of beer against the front of her blouse. Gasping in surprise, she wrapped her hands around his keeping the bottles in place, the freezing sensation flashing through her in counter point to the heat building in her belly. The cold and wet hardened her nipples, and a throbbing erupted deep inside.

Turning in his embrace, her gaze searched his face—for what? She didn't even know. *Just live in the moment, it's all you can count on.* Shifting the beers to one hand, he reached sideways and set them on the counter. The smoldering expression in his eyes said he remembered what it felt like to be deep inside of her—and he wanted to feel that way again. Roughly tugging his T-shirt free of his jeans, she stripped it up over his head, and ran one hand across his muscled chest. He seemed built for action, but the scars he carried said he'd maybe seen too much. Still, being a warrior, she guessed he didn't feel the same.

His hands framed her face, and he kissed her. Softly, gently, coaxing. No turning back now as his touch turned demanding. She responded in kind, reaching to unbutton her blouse. He still wanted her, and by Jupiter she wanted him—with enough heat to melt the ice caves of Epsilon-b.

The jolting and unwelcoming cry of both their cell phones barely penetrated brains fevered with only one intention. Reluctantly, Solace broke away first, and grabbed hers.

"Yes, Mother. Solace here." She tried not to gasp for breath as she shook off the haze of desire still intoxicating mind and body.

"Are you alone," Mother asked.

"No," she gulped. Dang caught again with Tanner when she should probably be reviewing some new information, or polishing her laser gun.

"Are you with Lieutenant Jackson?"

"Yes." She answered truthfully but cringed expecting a reprimand.

"Good," Mother continued, surprising the heck out of her. "There's been an assault on the NOAA facility. Not totally unexpected, but we thought we had more time. I'm guessing the failed attempt on Lieutenant Jackson sped up their agenda."

"Was Thompson in on it?" she asked, turning her back toward Tanner.

"It's a possibility, but I certainly hope not. We can't locate him." Mother sounded disappointed as if she'd been sure Thompson would co-operate for the good of the cause.

"What's the situation?" Solace asked.

"They've taken over the main level but haven't gained access to the Think Tank. So far all satellites appear intact and in proper orbit. For some reason, they don't appear to be trying to take over the building. A small blessing there. We also have confirmation they commandeered a drone."

"What the—" Solace caught herself before blurting out a typical human expletive.

"Exactly," Mother agreed.

Where the heck had the Reps gotten a drone? She glanced over her shoulder, her worried expression crashing headfirst into Tanner's.

"Go in fast and hard. We weren't expecting them,

and hopefully they won't be expecting the four of you. Portence and Bliss are already deployed."

"I'm on the way," she said, hearing the same words echo from across the room.

"I'll drive," he offered, hitching into his T-shirt and grabbing truck keys off the counter.

"I'll fly," she countered.

He stopped short and turned toward her. She lingered long enough to softly kiss him and then hurried on. "Meet you there," she called over her shoulder. "Stay safe."

Chapter Thirteen

Solace hovered for a split-second then landed beside a large fir tree.

Dematerializing her wings, she glanced around the NOAA parking lot. It appeared normal. No flashing red lights or Army vehicles circling the building. No choppers hovering overhead. Had she misunderstood regarding the Rep's attempted takeover?

"I know," Bliss whispered. "We thought there'd be more action, too."

Solace jumped. She'd been so intent on the scoping out the area, she hadn't felt her sisters' presence.

"It's designated a covert op," Port informed her, "so as not to upset the general population. It also eliminates any outside ground support."

Tanner's truck careened around the corner and skidded to a stop about ten yards away. Solace stepped into the open to gain his attention. He slipped out of the truck, his Jericho 941 in hand. Bent low, he crossed over to her, gently pushing her back into the cover of the foliage.

"We're on our own," he said, nodding recognition to Port and Bliss. "No one else on combat level has been briefed on who or what the Reps are. And we don't have time to instruct them."

"Fine with me," Port growled, adjusting her arm rings.

Bliss handed Solace a pair. She slipped them on. All three women checked the load on their particle lasers then activated the rings into spiked shields covering their forearms. When necessary the hardware they wore could morph into body armor, handy little trick, especially for a girl who liked bling.

Tanner shook his head. "Nice touch. What's the plan? We can't just go barging in there, bracelets jangling. The hostages could be harmed."

"You can't, but we can," Solace explained. She cloaked her image then reappeared.

"Damn," Tanner said, with a shake of his head. "Not sure I'll ever get used to that one."

"Well worry about it later, soldier boy," Port snapped. "We're going in."

Port and Bliss headed across the parking lot. She could still see them, but knew Tanner couldn't.

"Don't shoot one of us," Solace joked, skimming the fingers of one hand along his left cheek. "Even if you can't see us, we're not impervious to bullets."

"But—" Before he could finish the sentence, she followed her sisters.

The front door to NOAA stood wide open. The inside security door blown to bits. The guard she'd come to know lay dead on the floor in a pool of blood. No foul smell rent the air. Evidently none of the Reps had been killed or wounded.

As her sisters headed down the main hallway, she glanced back out the front window, watching Tanner as he worked his way across the lot between the parked cars. He paused at the main entrance. Knowing he would be right behind her, she followed Port and Bliss.

In the break-room, about eight NOAA employees

sat bound in chairs, one lay wounded on the floor by the coffee machine. They weren't killing indiscriminately. Rather unusual, as acts of mercy had never been the Reps strong suit. Maybe they didn't know if they might need someone at a later date.

Slipping by unseen, the trio moved on to check out the labs. Sounds of people calling for help echoed behind her, Tanner must have reached the bound employees. She knew he would stop to untie the workers. It crossed her mind to call 911 regarding the injured man but decided it was a choice that should be left up to Tanner.

The few employees in the second lab had put up a fight. They were all dead. Guess the Reps had run out of patience. Cabinet drawers were open, the contents spilling out, and most of the computers had been trashed. Rather than any kind of full-fledged takeover, the mission seemed to have degenerated into one of smash and grab. If they didn't reach the Reps before they destroyed the GPS tracking units, or stole them, the results would be just as bad as a takeover.

Screams came from the conference room up ahead. Solace and her sisters entered and spread out. Four Reps, in all their hideous glory, were trying to subdue the panicky employees. Hoping to avoid another bloodbath, Solace dropped her cover and fired at the closest monster. To remain cloaked took a tremendous amount of energy, and Solace needed all her strength and wits about her to maintain her wings and activate her arm protectors. Boxed in, she couldn't fly, but combat wings were good for deflection, and the metal-tipped talons could do damage on their own.

The terrified employees momentarily succumbed to

open-mouthed silence as the Reps turned their attention on the Faes. Then all hell broke loose. Portence blasted away, and green blood splattered one wall. Utilizing her laser, Solace tracked a wound straight across another Rep's neck. Decapitation and an ungodly smell soon followed. Bliss engaged two enemies who had been stacking computer files and equipment in a corner. Port went to help her.

The only other Rep appeared to be hiding by the outer wall. What the hector was he doing? Solace headed straight for him. Holy Mother, he was setting Semtex, a plastic explosive. Had they already planted more in the other rooms? She hadn't noticed. It made sense. No use taking over a building you really didn't need. Just blow it up. Using blasting caps or timers, they could set off a chain reaction large enough to wipe out not only the building, but the entire block. A laser hit to the compound could set it off too.

"Their using plastic," she hollered to warn her sisters. "Run," she yelled at the employees.

Coming to their senses, the workers hightailed it out of the room and back down the hall toward Tanner and safety. Which would be more than the workers in the underground lab could hope for if the building collapsed.

Holstering her laser, she launched herself at the Rep—and the explosives. Was he on a suicide mission? Was she? He saw her coming, and swinging his extended left arm backward, he clotheslined and stopped her cold. She hit the floor with a grunt of pain. Scrambling to her feet, she shook her head, tried to clear her senses. The Rep faced her full on, grinning, but not advancing. Luckily, the low ceiling restricted his tactical movements, allowing no space to swing his lethal tail. He just watched her, like he knew something she didn't. She reached for her laser. S*crew the sucker, and the explosives.* Before she could pull the trigger, the wall behind him exploded.

Debris rocketed past Solace. She hit the floor, hands over her sensitive ears. Daring to lift her head and squinting open her eyes, she peered through the haze of dust. Most of the wall remained intact, minus a ten by ten whole in the middle. Thank goodness Port and Bliss were across the room, and out of harm's way.

Returning defensive fire, the remaining Reps grabbed the computers files and other apparatus and fled through the opening to the outside.

Dematerializing her wings to accommodate the opening, she scrambled to her feet and followed on their scaly heels. The fresh air outside came as a relief, then a second explosion rocked the ground. It came from inside the building, and felt much bigger.

She turned back to check on her sisters. They weren't behind her, hadn't followed her out. They were still inside.

****

"Stay orderly, but don't stop," Tanner instructed, untying the last employee in the break room. The man by the coffee machine appeared dead, and he hoped the explosions they'd just heard would be limited to a salvo of two.

By his seat-of-the-pants count, about half the employees had been evacuated. He entered the hallway moving deeper into the building. As he turned a corner, another wave of people, all terrified eyes, gaping mouths, and churning feet came at him. These must be the lab geeks. One guy, being carried by two other men, left a spotty trail of blood along the way.

A third explosion rocked the building. Orderliness forgotten, screaming and running full tilt ensued, and with an *everyman for himself* attitude, the crowd headed for the front door. Tanner bucked the tide of frantic people, fighting his way in the opposite direction. He knew Solace and her sisters had come this way, he could smell them. He didn't know how or why, but when they were all together the air around them took on some kind of flowery scent.

Edging forward, dialing 911 as he went, he decided the potential for mass casualties now outweighed everything else. He'd be responsible for repercussions regarding bringing in outside personnel.

He barely got the directions relayed to the operator when a fourth blast hit. The floor shook, plaster cracked off the ceiling, and a gaping hole opened up at his feet, halting him in his tracks. Too wide to jump across, and with no handy material to use as a bridge, he couldn't get through to the back of the building. Frustrated, he kicked a pile of rubble out of the way and sprinted back the way he'd come.

While driving over, he'd snagged his camo bandana and hunting vest from behind the backseat and put them on. Now he yanked the bandana up over his nose so he could breathe as another blast followed in his wake filling the air with more dust. Soon there would be nothing left of this place.

A grim scene met him outside. Several employees held onto trees for support, coughing and weeping. Others lay in the grass or even on the concrete in the parking lot. Stepping around them, he tore the fabric from his face to suck in the clean air. Then he ran around toward the back of the building.

Bad leg throbbing, he skidded around the corner and stopped, staring at the back of the building. Rubble met his frantic gaze, rubble and little hope anyone inside could still be alive.

"I don't care, dammit," he growled, gripping the cell phone so tight it hurt his hand. "You track down General Harker, now. Tell him what I said, and send a full Army Disaster Recovery Team here on the double."

\*\*\*\*

Solace struggled but couldn't move. Someone carried her in strong arms, but *her* arms were tied to her sides, her ankles to one another, and the bag over her head blocked out all vision. What happened? She must have lost consciousness. She heard twigs snapping and the muffled sound of someone walking through underbrush. How long had she been out? And what about Bliss and Port. Were they okay?

Squirming, she tried to scrunch the bag up enough to see.

"Be still, or they'll zap you again," a deep voice growled in her ear.

Frick, the Reps had her. They probably hit her with some kind of stun gun when she'd turned to go back for her sisters. How long had she been out? Her muscles ached from being tied up, and from being shot through with electricity. Maybe she could conjure up a wind storm, but what if it did more harm than good. Concentrating harder, she tried again to reach her sisters. No luck. Tears wet her cheeks. They were finally back together, she couldn't lose them now.

Whoever carried her stopped, and she heard car

doors opening and closing. Then it sounded like the panel of a van sliding open. Dumped unceremoniously inside, she rolled onto her back and kicked out with her bound feet.

"Keep still," the voice warned again.

The engine started, the panel door slid shut, and the vehicle sped away, bouncing over rough terrain. They were off-road, and there were lots of places around Boulder where these jerks could be hiding out. She kept trying to reach her sisters, hoping Tanner had found them. Or maybe Tanner was in trouble, too.

Listening carefully, she tried to keep track of any element which might give her a clue as to where they were taking her. The receding traffic noise meant they were heading deeper into the foothills, the splash of water indicating they'd crossed a creek, which didn't narrow things down much. And keeping track of left and right turns soon became impossible.

Finally, the vehicle stopped, while others crunched to a halt nearby. Someone, roughly hauled Solace up and out of the van. They carried her inside a warm building where they untied and tossed her on the floor. A clanging noise followed, it rang with the ominous sound of a jail cell slamming shut. The smell of a wounded Rep made her gag.

Angry voices filtered over to her. She couldn't understand what they were saying, but it sounded like they were arguing amongst themselves. Snatching the bag from her head, she blinked and took stock of her surroundings. Two Reps looked ready to go for one another's throats. The third sat in a nearby chair, holding his thigh, groaning in pain.

Studying her surroundings in more detail, she

discovered they'd brought her to an abandoned warehouse. An image of "Mr. White" flashed through her mind. What was it with these guys and warehouses? At least this one appeared cleaner, and other than a few small odds and ends, nearly empty—except for the huge steel cage they'd locked her in.

Chapter Fourteen

Their covert operation had turned into a full-fledged catastrophe, just like his last mission, and Tanner felt just as helpless now as he did then. But Solace or her sisters weren't going to die on his watch.

"Solace," he hollered, "Solace can you hear me." She had lots of special "qualities". Maybe faerie ears were more sensitive than human ones. "Solace," he tried again as he tore at more of the debris. "Make a noise if you're in there."

To his relief and surprise, he heard a thumping sound coming from inside near the intact portion of the wall. Foraging nearby, he dragged a downed tree branch closer, using it to lever the heavier pieces of wreckage to one side. Clawing and tearing at the smaller rubble, he managed to create a basketball size hole to the inside, but when he pressed his face to the opening it was too dark to see anything.

"Hello," he called.

A flash of red hair caught his eye and Bliss' face appeared.

"Thank God you're alive. Are Portence and Solace with you?"

"I'm here soldier boy." Portence said, although her tough demeanor seemed a bit shaky.

"What about Solace," he asked again, his heart rate doubling as he waited for an answer. She had to be okay.

"Stop talking and keep digging," Portence ordered.

Deciding this wasn't the time to lock horns with Solace's sister, he did just that.

Soon the opening grew large enough to pull the two females to safety. He kept waiting for Solace to appear at the opening. When she didn't he turned to the sisters, fear coursing through him, their faces answering the question he didn't want to ask.

"She got out," Bliss explained, gently placing her hand on his arm, "right behind the Reps. Then the building collapsed and we couldn't follow."

"Then where is she?" he demanded, anger battled fear at the thought of Solace in the hands of the scaly creatures.

"We aren't sure," Bliss responded.

"At least the two of you look okay," he reasoned, checking them out. "No major signs of injury or bleeding."

"Almost." Bliss lifted the edge of her blouse. A stream of blue ran down her left side across her ribs to her waist. "I don't think it's as bad as it looks."

"Your blood is blue?" he sputtered, surprise momentarily eclipsing concern. "There's help on the way," he reassured. "They can take you to the hospital."

"No way," Bliss gritted, between clenched teeth as Portence wrapped her scarf around her midriff. "I've had worse, and we have to find Solace. Besides, only one hospital is set up to treat our kind, and it should remain unknown. If it's destroyed, there will be no one to help us should a really bad need arise."

Trusting the sisters knew best, at least on this matter, Tanner scouted the area for signs of what might have happened.

"I can feel Solace," Portence said, eyes closed, arms outstretched. "She's not too far away."

There's fresh tire tracks leading into the woods. I'll get the truck."

"We can fly." Port opened her eyes and glanced his way.

"One of you can," he reasoned. "And if Solace is hurt we may need the truck to bring her to that special hospital of yours. No arguments," he barked, as Portence opened her mouth to speak.

"I was going to say," she snapped back, "I agree."

**** 

Solace grabbed the bars of the cage door and rattled the panel as hard as she could. Rage bolstered her strength, but not enough to do any damage to the enclosure. At least it made her feel better.

"Stop all the racket," the largest Rep snarled at her. "When Mr. Smith gets here, you'll wish you could stay in there."

That didn't sound good. "Screw you," she flung back at him, stepping away from the bars. Smith must be the leader of their nasty little group.

She took a deep breath and tried to calm down, tried to think of a plan for when Smith arrived. It didn't take long to realize she had few options. In an attempt to aggravate her captors, she materialized a small set of wings and flew to the top of the cage. Hovering there she checked it for structural weakness, but found none. Drifting back to the ground, she opened her senses trying to reach her sisters again. She'd barely begun when their response nearly bowled her over. They must have gotten out, they were free, they were heading this way. But what about Tanner? She had no way of communicating with him. Her sisters ratcheted down their search power to normal capacity, they knew her location.

The wounded Rep hobbled over to a bed and dropped down onto the mattress. Although not decapitated, he still stunk to high heaven. When her sisters got close enough, they could probably hone in on the stench. Her gaze drifted around the facility. There were weapons stacked by the door. Evidently, holing up here after hitting NOAA had been prearranged. A refrigerator stood in one corner, near a table and chairs. The walls to the building appeared to be cement blocks, thick and sturdy. Taking this place wouldn't be easy.

The two uninjured Reps hurried over to a window. Something must be going on outside. *Please don't let it be Mr. Smith,* she prayed. The two started arguing again. Good—dissention in the enemy ranks never hurt. Her sisters were very close, she could feel them without even trying. Hopefully they had gotten here before Smith. The largest Rep fished a cell phone from a backpack, but all she heard from this end was "*Yes sir. Yes sir.*" And when he hung up he started handing out weapons.

The smaller Rep edged closer to her cage. Now what, a little last minute bullying before Mr. Big arrived? "Take a good look," she taunted, going into full combat mode, spike tipped wings and all. "Your scaly ass is grass. The whole U.S. Army is on its way. You don't stand a chance of getting out of here alive."

He didn't seem impressed with her lie. He just blinked twice and kept staring at her. Something about this Rep caught her attention. His eyes were green-tinged, not dead black like the others. The oddness of it left her mute.

"Don't be afraid," he said, in the same voice she'd heard when being carried.

Before she could fathom what he meant, or respond, someone blasted away at the front door with what had to be a particle laser. Way to go Bliss. But the reinforced door held. Then she felt Port above her. She'd landed on the roof. The wounded Rep and the bigger one busted out a front window, firing back just like a shootout in the old west.

The door to the building began to smolder. Bless those particle lasers. The two Reps who had been returning fire gave up and began packing the stolen computer files and equipment, moving them to the back of the building.

"Get over here Thompson."

She gave a start and glared at the creature standing in front of her cage. "I knew you were a friggin' Rep the day I met you in the lab, you stinking son of a lizard."

"Actually, I'm only half stinking lizard." He sounded almost wistful. "My mom was a Reptilian. My father human—whoever he was."

A Manimal—which explained the green eyes. Contemplating the implications, Solace remained silent while an image of Mr. Spock flashed through her mind. Half human/half Vulcan, but he was a nice guy and much better looking than Thompson. Or could it be a load of flying cosmic donkey dung.

He unlocked the cage door.

She stepped back out of reach, wondering what he had in mind. He'd never fit through the door, but she'd sure be better off outside this cage. Dematerializing her wings, she streaked through the small opening, past him, and into the middle of the warehouse. The swooshing sound of a tail whipping through the air came too late.

Knocked off her feet, she landed flat on her back, reeling from where her head hit the cement floor. Before she could get up, a large lizard foot came down on her chest, knocking the wind out of her as she stared up at the SIG-SAUR 9mm clutched in his huge hand.

"You Fae bitches are sure hard to kill," the big Rep snarled. "But you're not going to make it out alive this time." He grinned down at her, spittle dripping from his pointy teeth.

Activating her arm rings, she stabbed the Rep's ankle with the four-inch spike protruding from the cuff. He yelped and raised his foot enough for her to slide out from under it. Free and really pissed, she wished she had her particle laser. This would all be over in a galactic flash.

With a battle cry meant to shock the Rep and give her strength, she morphed into full combat mode, growing larger, more muscular. Tattoos and eyes glowing, she created a whirlwind, the blast of air tumbling the table and chairs like children's toys as it blew out the glass windows still intact.

His tail came around again. Ready this time she hovered out of the way. He held his position from across the room, and calmly took aim at her. She took evasive action as best she could, but held little hope of out maneuvering a bullet. Then Thompson tackled the bigger Rep knocking him to the ground. They wrestled and rolled like monsters gone mad. Dust flying, howls of pain and anger filling the air.

Thompson appeared to be losing the fight, and the wounded Rep looked ready to join the fray. Doubting he would aid Thompson's cause, she gain altitude and torpedoed Rep number three, feet first. Reeling from the hit, he collapsed backward, screaming in pain, clutching at his thigh wound now reopened and gushing green blood.

She raced to the front door. Locked and too hot to handle. As she turned away, Tanner kicked it in from the outside. He leaped through the opening, Bliss close behind. Port dropped down from a hole in the roof. Thompson huddled on the floor, oozing green from a myriad of cuts, but just as the larger Rep made good his original plan to shoot her, Thompson staggered to his feet and threw himself in front of her, taking the bullet with her name on it. Stunned by the act of bravery, she hurried to his side as Tanner, Bliss, and Port finished off the remaining two Reptiles.

Kneeling beside Thompson, she tried to staunch the blood pouring from his chest wound.

"Tell Mother I'm sorry," he gritted, between clenched teeth.

"Stay with me," she ordered, "you're going to make it."

"No, I'm done for. But it's okay. I never fit in with the Reptiles or the humans. At least Mother gave me a chance to make a difference."

"I promise, I'll let her know," she assured him. If Thompson hadn't blocked the shot, she would be the one bleeding out.

## Chapter Fifteen

As evening shadows deepened, Tanner insisted on carrying Bliss all the way up to the penthouse apartment. Solace and Portence followed on his heels.

"Put her here on the couch," Solace instructed.

"Are you sure she'll be okay," he asked, his brow furrowed with concern.

"We have a slew of medical supplies," Port insisted. "And we heal fast. Thank you for not leaving us behind and going after Solace alone."

Her show of gratitude came as a surprise. "You're welcome," he said quietly.

Today's events had hit him hard. Seeing their enemy in reptile form had been a revelation bordering on a shock, making everything he'd been told all too real. They were huge, hideous, and a tactical nightmare. Losing those employees and the guard also sparked into life memories which always lay smoldering in the back of his mind. "We're a team," he added, "that means nobody ever gets left behind."

"Tanner," Solace said, laying a hand on his arm. She nodded toward the balcony. He joined her outside, and she closed the sliding door, giving them some privacy.

"Bliss is going to be okay," she reassured him.

"If you say so."

"I do. So what's really bothering you?"

He hadn't meant to let her zone in on his mood, but since she had, it would be good to get a few things out in the open.

"I'm part of the team now, right. But earlier today you three just went off without me. I didn't know where any of you were, or if you were okay."

"I'm sorry we didn't think about it from your side. Look, we each have different skill sets and training, and even gut instinct. Sometimes that's going to have us approaching the same situation from a different perspective and prompting a different response. If we'd all been attached at the hip today, we'd probably still be in the rubble waiting to be rescued.

"Instead, you saved my sisters, and the three of you saved me. I'd say that's pretty darn good teamwork. I know you're accustomed to being the leader, being in charge. But it's different now. We're all equal on this team, which means no one individual is more responsible than the next guy for the outcome, successful or otherwise, or for casualties or anything else. Capisce?"

He smiled at her use of slang and had to admit her little speech did ease the blame he seemed so good at heaping upon himself. Still... "You don't understand," he began, then hesitated. His last mission overseas had been a total cock-up. And regardless of why or whose fault it was, he'd been in charge. He didn't believe in passing the buck. But telling Solace and her sisters about the mission might lower their confidence in him as a soldier. Not good for the group as a whole. And although, if need be he would die for Solace, he didn't trust her—not with his heart. That organ might just be more spiritually broken than the rest of his body was physically wrecked.

"Mother wouldn't have given you to us if she didn't have complete faith in your honor and your skills."

She slipped her arms around his neck and pressed her body close. "So, you don't have to tell me anything. Your General Sherman had it right when he said *men think that war is all glamour and glory, but let me tell you, boys, it is all Hell!* It was then, it is now, and it always will be," she added.

Wrapping his arms around her, he held on for dear life, feeling comfort rather than arousal. Sweet comfort, a sense of wellbeing so long missing in his life. Knowing they could share moments like this, and not just mind-blowing sex, made him feel even closer to her. His shoulders relaxed. She made him whole again. Solace had said all the right things, and he truly thought she meant them. How could such a tough little ET feel so soft in his arms?

He eased back and studied her beautiful face, losing his troubles in those light green eyes.

"You're correct," he said. "And just so we're all on equal footing as far as what demons run loose in our brains, for me the past starts today. And it's what we do together from here on out that counts."

Portence slid the door open and poked her head out. "Hey you two. Bliss and I are hitting the racks. Just wanted to say goodnight, and here—" Her last words were followed by her tossing an object in Solace's direction.

"Saw you favoring your shoulder a few times today, Tanner. This should help, and yes we've got plenty so you won't be taking any away from Bliss."

With a grin she closed the door.

Solace held a tube of ointment called Saturnalia Cream.

"Is it really made on Saturn?"

"No. It's from Kepler 186f, my planet. It's beautiful there," she added, "and resembles Earth more than any place I've seen." She wiggled the tube. "They just wanted a fancy otherworldly name for the ointment because it smells and looks like coal tar. But it works."

"Take off your shirt," she ordered, opening the tube of ointment.

"Yes, sir, or ma'am, or—what rank are you anyway?" he asked.

When she ran a hand across his chest, warm feelings of wellbeing skyrocketed to arousal, making him lose his train of thought.

"I'm a lieutenant too, in the Alpha Warrior Squadron."

He just smiled.

"What," she demanded.

"Nothing."

"Really, what?"

"Just never thought I'd find a female who would understand what makes a soldier tick. Or what makes one stop ticking on occasion."

She nodded in understanding then spread the black goo on his scarred shoulder, front and back. When she finished, she kissed his chest, right over his heart, and he swore he felt it down to his toes. A sweet gesture, not sexy, and again he marveled at their capacity to relate on different levels.

"Now put your shirt on, and get out of here, you big palooka. No way you're getting in my bed smelling like a Hydra goat." She screwed the cap back on the ointment and handed him the tube. "Wait 24 hours before using more," she added, "and don't put heat on the area."

"Yes, doctor," he teased, shrugging into his shirt, "whatever you say. I'm thinking I might need a follow up appointment as soon as possible."

"Of course. We have very flexible hours. Just give us a call."

She escorted him to the front door of the apartment, and although tired and sore, he wished he could spend the night. But they had both been through a lot. He needed to get down on disc exactly what had happened today, she probably needed to do the same, and he could barely keep his eyes open.

Taking her lead, he gave her a friendly kiss on the mouth, leaving quickly before his desire to do and say more ruined his hopefully gallant exit.

****

Solace lay in bed, aching in body and soul. A dip in the hot tub had sounded nice, but also like too much effort, so she just stared at the ceiling as she tried to sort out her emotions. She really liked Tanner, and it seemed obvious he liked her. But what kind of a future could they have? Giving up being a Fae Warrior wouldn't even register in her brain, which meant she could be transferred to another planet at any time.

Besides, even if she became a Fae civilian, it didn't mean she would be allowed to live on the Earth. There were planetary restrictions. And if by some chance Tanner wanted to follow her to her home planet, it seemed a doubtful dream. There were beings and entities other than Fae on her plant, so granted by the

Council, but for obvious reasons, no humans. If only living in the moment came more easily to her like it did for Bliss, the free-spirit/free-love sister. Or maybe she should break the tie now, not let things go any further, and be alone like Port.

A little voice in the back of her mind protested a big *No* to both options. Caught in the middle again, she could neither give him up, nor give her heart without hoping for a future.

Talking to him as a friend had been wonderful, although what they shared sexually went beyond wonderful to spectacular. Still it was nice to know he liked her for other reasons, and seemed to have gotten over the not-of-this-realm hurdle.

Her thoughts kaleidoscoped across her mind. Finally overtaken by exhaustion, she snuggled down under the covers. Just as she drifted off, her phone rang. She lurched sideways and grabbed it up off the nightstand.

Tanner! No longer sleepy, pulse racing, she hit answer.

"Hi. Everything okay?"

"Just wanted to let you know, all the employees in the underground lab made it out alive prior to the building collapsing. Someone up top hit the silent alarm, giving them time to block the main door to their area and escape out the underground tunnel system. They took backup equipment, too."

She breathed a sigh of relief. She felt so sorry about some of the lab workers being killed. Believing the rest of those poor people had died underground had been weighing heavily on her. Dying without a fighting chance was no way to go.

"Thanks. I'm glad to hear it. Are you home already?" She conjured a picture of him at his house, stripped down to his boxers. Running her hand down the front of her body, she wondered what picture teased through his mind.

"Yes. I'm just about to hit the hay. Thanks for the smelly cream, it's helping quite a bit."

"You're welcome. Too bad it doesn't taste better, I would have insisted you stay, and then licked it off of you."

A choking sound filtered though from the other end.

"You still there?" she asked.

"Oh, yes, I'm here. And now, thanks to you, I'll never get any sleep tonight."

"Good. Talk to you soon."

With a wicked smile, she hung up. Always leave them wanting more.

Chapter Sixteen

"Who is it?" Port asked, speaking into the intercom beside the entrance to the penthouse.

"Concierge, with the food you ordered."

Port clapped her hands in glee before opening the door. "Would you put it by the table please?" Like a hound on the scent, she trailed the young man as he pushed the food-laden cart across the room. "Thank you," she added, handing him a tip as he passed her on his way back out the door.

"This is why I thought it would be more fun to meet here this morning rather than at your place," Solace explained to Tanner.

"Can't argue with you there," he agreed, eyeing the mound of bagels, scrambled eggs, and fresh fruit accompanied by coffee, tea, and a pitcher of juice. "I assume the sausages are for me," he said, reaching for and taking the entire plate. "One good thing about hanging out with vegetarians." As they sat around the table, Solace, Port, and Bliss wasted no time digging in as well.

"So," Solace said, around a mouthful of bagel. "Mother has located the Mr. Smith I heard the Reps talking about at the warehouse. They sounded in awe of him, so we have to figure he's a big shot in this whole operation." She stopped talking to take a sip of coffee, then distribute the documents Mother had messengered over earlier.

"He's got an office in Boulder, a shell company called The Priselet Corporation. They make and repair corporate high-tech security systems. My guess is they're also experts at fouling them up, drumming up business in buildings they'd like to have a peek at. It also gives them cover to play with all types of gadgets and gizmos without raising eyebrows. I played around with the letters in the fake company name, you'll notice Priselet is an anagram for Reptiles—the arrogant bastards."

"It says here," Bliss read, "the whereabouts of Mr. Smith's private residence is unknown. That means taking him down at home is not an option. Also, the building where his office is located houses a huge daycare center, so storming the workplace during the day won't do either."

"We could try a stop and snatch where he parks his car," Tanner suggested.

"Might work," Solace agreed, "but apparently he travels with a full complement of body guards. Things could get messy in a hurry for all concerned. Don't worry," she added, handing out invitation cards. "Mother's planned a fundraiser at a nearby country club. Most people invited will be agents from the task force you're working with Tanner. You'll only have four more days training time, but the party is probably our best chance to isolate and take him down. If we're lucky, we eliminate some of the Reps working for him."

"What makes you think he'll show?" Tanner asked.

"It's being hosted by the Chamber of Commerce, and Priselet Corp. will be receiving an award for best new company. Also there will be lots of eye-candy, young women from an up and coming modeling agency handing out the drinks and printed material."

"Is it formal, do we get to dress up?" Bliss cut in.

"Always the fashionista," Port teased. "I'd rather work behind the scenes, so I can wear my leather jumpsuit."

"Sounds the perfect setup," Solace agreed. "Especially since you still haven't heard from your contact in Colorado Springs. You won't have an escort."

"Don't rub it in," Port bristled. "This mystery man has a butt-load of bad manners to make up for, and the list is growing."

"You could at least wait to hear his side," Bliss encouraged. "Or maybe the cats out of the bag down there too about us, and your reputation for disliking human males has preceded your arrival. He's probably afraid to meet you."

"Why should he care one way or the other whether or not I liked humans, regardless of gender? This is a job, a mission. Unlike the two of you, I'm not here to fall in love."

Solace cringed, not daring to look at Tanner.

Bliss took offense. "Why do you insist on hating love?" she asked, sadness reflected in her eyes.

"I don't hate love," Port defended, "I hate love being blind. Or more accurately, love making you blind."

"To answer your question, Bliss," Solace interrupted, in an effort to stop all the talk about love, "yes, it's formal."

She needed to get everybody back on track.

Besides, personal conversation shouldn't be so readily shared in front of an outsider. Thinking of Tanner in those terms came as a bit of a shock. But Port's mission-first attitude made Solace reconsider her recent behavior. It seemed a bit careless and cavalier. Yet, she couldn't help how she felt about Tanner, or how she felt when with him. But neither of them had said anything about love.

"If needed, Mother has two tux on standby, one for Tanner and one for Bliss' partner, Mr. Calhoun," she said, forging on.

"Nathaniel will look gorgeous in a tux," Bliss purred.

"You'll be pretty too," Solace jibed at Tanner, trying to lighten the mood.

"Great," he nodded, "one more thing I can cross off my bucket list." He flipped through the readout. "Anything in here about the dead prostitutes and those other women?"

"No," Solace admitted, with a shake of her head. "But it's got to be the Reps. We should try and get a sample of Smith's DNA at the party. As far as we know there aren't any female Reps on Earth so…" She let the statement hang, trying not to think about what those women had endured.

"Since the Reps are such scumbags, I don't like the idea of any more young women being used as bait at the party." Tanner's expression hardened and a muscle jumped in his cheek as he clenched his jaw.

"They should be experienced enough to keep it professional. And with all your undercover agents on hand, they'll be safer with us than out there alone."

"I hope so," he relented. "I'm looking forward to

taking out more of those huge piss ants. Other than for Thompson's fleeting show of concern for you, they seem devoid of any redeeming qualities."

"Thompson came through in the end, that's for sure," Port said.

"Guess the human part of him won out over the reptile genes. That's kinda reassuring." Solace owed her life to him. "And I think it meant a great deal to him that he died with honor."

"Too bad the Universe didn't get rid of these butt-ugly monsters long ago," Tanner growled.

"To be more specific, it's the Multiverse," Solace corrected, "and it hasn't been for lack of trying. The Reps have survived for millions of years on their own. And now they're even more dangerous. They didn't bankroll this invasion. They're the muscle, answering to another entity."

"And who might that be?" Tanner asked.

"We aren't sure, but it's someone bent on taking over not only the earth, but the whole planetary sector. The Reps view destruction as entertainment, without a master plan. To put it in Earth terms, they're like medieval people with nuclear weapons. Their sensibilities haven't caught up with the technology they've been given. Perhaps it never will. They really aren't built for it. The lizard part of their brain is dominant, leaving little or no room for conscience or sentiment. And having once lived on Earth, I'm afraid they think they're coming home. Which is no doubt why they were used. Revenge is a great motivator, and an even more formidable enemy."

"Also makes for just as much of a dead one," he reassured, "once my men are up to speed."

"How's the training going?" Port asked.

"It's a good group. They were pre-screened to make sure they could handle the alien twist in this mission. But they were only told of the Reps, not you guys, not the Fae. One step at a time, I guess. Not all the men made the cut. It's a lot to swallow. There are days it's still hard for me to take it all in."

"And how are things going now back at NOAA?" Bliss asked.

"The majority of employees and salvaged equipment have been moved to another location. They'll be on lockdown during the day, and heavily guarded at night. Another strike is unlikely, which means the Reps will probably move on to a new target."

"Did the attack destroy any of the satellites, or disrupt the GPS systems?" Solace asked.

"No. So they're back to square one regarding either goal. Another reason for them to move on to try and make headway in another venue."

They sat in silence. Solace figured they would try for the cesium clock before taking on Cheyenne Mountain. Apparently the others thought so too as all gazes now turned toward Bliss.

"Let's not jump to conclusions," Bliss said. "There are lots of other targets. Don't get me wrong," she added. "I'm as anxious as anybody to kick some scaly derriere, but Nathaniel seems like such a sweet guy. I hate to see him mixed up in this thing."

"You'll be there to keep an eye on him," Solace encouraged. "And you'll have him all to yourself on Friday night."

"What are you wearing, Solace," Bliss asked. "I'm thinking pale lavender."

"That would be gorgeous with your red hair," Solace nodded. "I'm leaning toward…

"I'm out of here," Tanner said, standing and gathering his copies of the latest Intel. "Thanks for breakfast."

"You don't want to know what I'll be wearing?" Solace asked, trying hard to work her mouth into a pout. She never pouted, but thought she'd give it a try.

"Surprise me. See you guys at the country club"

"What's the matter," Port hassled, "afraid to get in touch with your feminine side?"

"More afraid of seeing yours," Tanner threw back, beating a hasty retreat.

"I like him," Port admitted, after he left. "Yeah, yeah, I know," she added at Solace and Bliss' stunned expressions. "But it doesn't mean I've changed my mind regarding dating Humes."

"Your loss," Solace teased.

Chapter Seventeen

Bliss fastened the last button on the back of Solace's red dress. Then she swirled around in a cloud of pale lavender while Port buckled the remaining straps on her leather jumpsuit.

As if on cue, they grinned at one another and simultaneously activated their wings, laughing with delight as they checked to see what each had chosen. Bliss modeled a pair of paper thin lavender minnies, artfully highlighted with veins of Spring green. Port went for full blown battle mode, but with spikes of gold, and the surprising and whimsical addition of a tetra-pound of glitter. But Solace stole the show with her unique mid-size wings of black lace. Technically of no use, and difficult to conjure.

"Oh, Solace. They're beautiful." Bliss reached out then drew back as if she thought they might be too fragile to touch. "Why haven't we tried lace before?"

"It's tricky," Solace admitted, holding her breath, "and hard to maintain." She gasped trying not to let go, but relaxing just a tiny bit, the lace disintegrated, followed by a collective *aaawww*.

Bliss and Port dematerialized theirs as well.

"Too bad we can't wear them to the party," Bliss said, with a sigh.

"This is sure one ridiculous way to wage a war," Port lampooned. "Going to parties instead of battlefields. We were trained for combat not ballroom dancing."

"Oh Port, I know you're not really hoping for all-out war," Solace warned.

"You're right. Sorry, I take it back, but I just want to get on with it, cold war tactics and covert ops are so restrictive, they make me edgy."

"Well cheer up. With any luck you and Bliss will have a chance to crack a few skulls tonight. But remember, if at all possible we need Smith alive. The holding cell at Fae HQ is ready and waiting."

"We better hit the road." Bliss glanced at the silver watch on her wrist.

"I'll drive," Port offered, as they took the elevator to the underground parking. "I can drop you guys off, park, and then slip in the back of the building. I'll take up position at one of the observation posts we decided on earlier today while reconnoitering."

"Works for me," Solace agreed. "Dang I feel naked without my laser, but we sure don't have a place to pack them in these outfits."

"I know," Bliss called from the backseat. "I feel the same way."

"Don't worry," Port reassured, "I'll be close enough to get them to you should the need arrive. I've also got a few other toys in my bag."

"What are you up to?" Solace gave her sister a nudge with her elbow.

"You'll just have to wait and see," Port hedged.

"We're a tad early," Solace noted as they eased to a stop in front of the country club. "How about, once inside, we do another sweep for bugs and explosives? And make sure the cameras are still in place."

"Good idea," Port called, waiting as the other two exited the car. "You and Bliss can nonchalantly handle the main party area and ladies room. I'll take the kitchen, cloak room, and service entrance. Catch you later."

"What's the matter, Solace," Bliss asked, as Port drove off.

"Nothing. I'm just so glad we're all together." Despite their ability to psychically connect to one another, she didn't like it when they were separated. After the explosion in the NOAA facility, she had an almost unreasonable fear of losing one of her sisters.

"We know how to take care of business, and each other," Bliss said, homing in on her thoughts. "We're like the Justice League, or the Avengers, only all-female. We need a name," she said, her voice almost giddy with excitement.

Solace smiled, took her by the arm, and led her toward the front door of the country club. "You and your superhero comics. We have a name, Fae Warriors Alpha Sector."

"But that's the name of everybody in Mother's elite force. We need a name for just the three of us."

"Okay. You work on a catchy name as we do the sweep. You better make it sound tough, or Port's not going to go for it."

"Good point"

They split off in different directions, weaving in and out of the wait-staff scurrying around with last minute setup chores. When the sound of high pitched female giggling leaked through the adjourning wall, Solace paused and opened the door a crack. Must be the models.

She peeked in the room. Was this some kind of cosmic joke? They were much younger than she expected, dressed in halter tops, short-shorts, and hooker heels. The *Chamber of Commerce* banner across each chest did little to calm the ocean of nubile cleavage. She'd bet a week's vacation on Paradise 5 Mother didn't know the models were barely more than teenagers.

The younger girls probably worked for less. Or they did it as a freebee with high hopes of making connections and becoming the next supermodel. Fighting the urge to pursue the issue and track down the person in charge of the agency, she moved on. Being in "guest mode", she had to let it slide. Causing a scene would be counterproductive, but you could bet she'd make sure someone heard about it later.

Finished with her sector, she slipped the tiny scanner back in her purse and waited to meet up with Bliss. A moment later, the lights went low, and the string quartet nestled in the balcony began tuning up and settling in for the duration. Guests began arriving in couples, milling about the room. None of the men fit the Smith's description.

"Everything checked out okay," Bliss reported, easing up to her side. "How about Dangerous Divas."

"Okay here too, and no-way will Port go for being called a Diva."

"Fatal Fems"

"That's even worse. Fatal Fems sounds like we're all dead, or we go around knocking off our dates. Speaking of which there's Tanner."

He stood just inside the door, tall, broad-shouldered, and magnificent in his tux. It might not be his preferred attire, but he carried it off like that James Bond guy she'd read about in the *History of American Theater and Films*. A pleasurable flutter skipped through her belly and dipped lower, and she wished she could conjure those black lace wings. Maybe later.

He spotted her, his gaze devouring her from top to bottom and back up again. He looked so serious. For a moment her confidence waned, then a lazy, sexy smile eased into place, and the heat in his eyes told her all she needed to know.

Adrenalin shot through her, and she imagined him removing her dress later. Regardless of circumstance or setting, Tanner made her feel as if she were either ready to do battle or make love, all senses on alert, heart pounding, boundless energy coiled in her belly.

He gave a little nod, but being a good soldier, put personal desire aside and skirted the area checking the perimeter rather than taking a direct path to her side. Bliss spotted Nathaniel, and with a sigh of delight made a beeline for him.

A hand slipped around her waist from behind. Wow, that was quick. She hadn't even heard Tanner coming, and with Fae ears that was quite a feat. A blanket of cold rather than heat enveloped her as tepid breath hovered at the nape of her neck. "You look good enough to eat, you delicious Fae morsel."

She stiffened, spun around, and took a hasty step backward. Smith...she'd been made. The Reps must be working off photo ID's just like they were.

"Be careful what you wish for, Mr. Smith," she returned, ignoring the deadly insult. "I met one of your associates with a similar appetite. I believe his name was Mr. White. Now he's eating dirt. I'd be glad to arrange for you join him."

Smith's smile faltered and contorted into a nasty sneer. Nearby, several hulking men stood strategically placed. Were they Tanner's men or Smith's?

Tanner stepped to her side and casually draped his arm across her shoulders indicating she belonged to him. "I see you've brought quite the entourage," he said, looking at Smith, but alerting her to whose side the brutes were on.

"Yes, one never knows what danger lurks in the most innocent of settings. Or what innocents tread unaware of the danger surrounding them."

Catching his double meaning, her gaze followed his to the small group of young models. He had to be the Rep killing the women. Only a higher up would be granted such a dangerous luxury. And the wretch had the balls to actually advertise the fact he was trolling for women, or in this case girls. But throwing out challenges and trying to ruffle her wings wasn't going to sidetrack her from her mission.

Tanner bristled. And Smith's body guards grinned and flexed as if cruising for a fight, too. She glanced over at the door leading to the cloakroom and spotted Port. When her sister cocked her head as if waiting for the signal to attack, Solace gave a little shake of her head and glanced away.

She leaned slightly closer to Tanner trying to ease the tactical response she figured he ached to unleash. They'd lost the element of surprise. An altercation now would be a bloody horror. But having a go at Smith outside sounded like a good option.

"Why don't we talk on the veranda?" she suggested. "Compressing your normal form into one more visually acceptable must make you uncomfortably warm."

At her insult, Smith's expression hardened, and his eyes flashed red. "In either guise, I'm superior to a Fae do-gooder out to save the earth."

"It's less worthy of saving since your kind arrived. But it's the only planet we have," Tanner threw at him.

"A pity you feeble humans are limited in your viability. But it also makes you much more compliant. You'll be slaves by the time this is over."

"A bunch of lunk-headed lizards won't be our masters. Or are you referring to the person who's really in charge of all this. The person you answer to?"

Solace involuntarily cringed. Calling a Rep a lizard really pissed them off.

Smith shuttered with rage, and she thought he might transform right before their eyes, but he seemed to catch himself just in time. About to suggest for the second time they go outside, the words were cut off when one of the young models rushed into the room, this time not giggling.

"They're gone," the girl blurted.

Solace's heart tripped forward double time, knowing without asking some of the models had been snatched. Fists clenched, she turned back toward Smith and glared at him.

"Don't look at me. I've been under your watchful eye the whole time."

She hurried over to the girl, Tanner at her side. "What happened," she asked, taking the girl by the arm and leading her over to Port. Standing nearby, Bliss quickly made excuses to Mr. Calhoun before joining them.

"Three of my friends are missing."

"How do you know this? Maybe they're just in another section of the club, handing out printed material."

"But that's just it. We were to take a few minutes to get familiar with the ballroom then meet in the conference room and pick up the flyers and leaflets. Once the party was in full swing, we were to start handing them. They never showed up. We were told never to leave those two areas."

The young woman began to shake. There had to be more to the story to upset her so much.

"What else," Solace prompted. "You won't get in trouble. Just tell us what you know."

"A man told some of us he was scouting for pretty young women to be in a music video."

"Is that him over there," Solace nodded toward Smith.

"No," the girl said, frantically looking around. "I don't see him anywhere in here. Oh, I told them not to go. I told them."

"Not to go where?"

"To the parking lot, near the trees. He said the video would mostly be shot at night, and he wanted to see if the camera loved them in shadow. I told them it sounded too good to be true. They wouldn't listen."

"It's not your fault." She put a comforting arm around the nearly hysterical model. "I need you to find the other girls still here. Stay in one group, find the person who runs the agency, and don't leave the building. Can you do that for me?"

The girl nodded.

Solace grabbed the particle laser Port offered.

"I've just checked in with my men," Tanner said, slipping the hand held back in his pocket. "A few were decoyed out of the main room when a smoke bomb went off near the loading dock behind the kitchen. And there's three I can't reach. Nobody knows where they are."

"Not hard to guess who's behind all this," Solace said, turning to confront Smith.

He was gone, along with his scaly goons. As Solace wondered how their plans had so quickly deteriorated, another smoke bomb went off. This time in the main ballroom. With memories of the recent explosions at NOAA fresh in their minds, the guests began evacuating the building in droves. And when they reached their cars and tried to leave all at once, chaos ruled.

Heading for the area by the trees where the models supposedly were, Solace spotted one of the missing special agents. He lay on the ground, and he'd been torn apart. Tanner's men were trained to give their all or die trying, and that's just what this soldier had done.

"How did the son-of-a-bitch have time to make such elaborate plans?" Tanner growled. Seething with anger, he glanced around seeking the other two men on his task force who had gone MIA.

"He seemed to know all along it was a set up. Let's fan out and search the area," she said to Port and Bliss.

Tanner nodded and fell in line.

A pine forest and hilly terrain ringed the northwest side of the country club making the going slow. But it didn't take long to find the second agent. He turned out to be luckier than his companion. Although in bad shape, he would probably pull through. Her heart ached knowing Tanner would agonize over the loss of one man and the wounding of another. He left the dog tags on the second man, but still held the first set in his fist. Stomach queasy, she thought about what awaited the models if they weren't located in time.

Reaching an open area with a narrow dirt road leading west, they found fresh tire tracks. The size and depth of the marks indicated a large vehicle, probably a 4x4. They had come this way all right. Blood glistened on the grass edging the road, and a small, woman's purse lay nearby.

"I can't find Jeffers," Tanner said, as they searched the immediate area for more information.

"Who?" she asked.

"Andy Jeffers," he repeated. "He's my third missing man. I don't know whether to be relieved in not finding him here, or even more upset. He's just a little guy, a NOAA employee, the only civilian in the group. He wanted to be on the team as retribution for losing a friend in the previous attack. He reminds me of Ralphie."

"Maybe he's not dead. Maybe the Reps have him."

"They wouldn't want extra baggage."

"Unless they thought they could use him somehow. Did he have any special training?"

Tanner gave a little shrug. "He's a geek. Good with computers and nanotechnology."

"Did he know anything about drones?"

The expression on Tanner's face said it all.

Chapter Eighteen

"I'll do an aerial recon," Bliss said, deploying battle wings and taking off.

"Port," Solace called. "Let's contact Mother."

Port hurried to her side, dropped the canvas duffle she toted, and dug the direct-link communicator from its depths.

"What's up ladies? Must be trouble if you're linking."

"Smith figured we were setting him up," Solace began. "And he not only got away clean, he took three of the models. Those poor girls, I'm sorry to report, were barely more than teenagers."

"By the gods," Mother swore.

Solace mirrored Port's look of surprise. Mother didn't often lose her cool. Somebody was going to feel her wrath.

"We've just located the place he's renting, he's probably heading there." Now Mother's voice sounded a little too controlled. "It's a house with a large equestrian set up, situated on forty acres."

"Directions," Port said, loading the information into her handheld.

"It's between the country club golf course and Boulder Reservoir. Heading north from your location, it's on 55th street, the first dirt road on your left after you cross Little Dry Creek. Supposedly there aren't any horses there at this time, but that's not confirmed."

"I hope that's true," Port said, "or the Reps would probably eat them. Unfortunately," she added, "that only leaves the models for them to snack on."

"We'd still like to take Smith alive," Mother advised, ignoring Port's comment and staying on point. "But the possibility seems less and less likely, and you have permission to do whatever is necessary to rescue those young women. He probably won't talk anyway. Stay safe. Mother out."

Tanner razed a hand across his face, muffling an expletive. "I'll meet you guys there."

He turned to leave, but Port held him back. "There's too much equipment in the back of Solace's car for me to carry while flying. Can we haul it in your truck?"

"Sure. I parked right next to you."

"You go find Bliss," Port suggested to Solace. "Tanner and I will meet you there."

"Okay," Solace agreed.

Port tucked the link away in the canvas bag. Solace placed her fingertips on each side of Port's face, Port did the same to her. Eyes closed they hummed, creating a unique sound frequency, a pathway for reaching one another, it couldn't be hacked, and would last until they reversed the procedure.

Opening her eyes, she met Port's gaze. *Be safe, sister mine*, they willed to one another.

Solace shifted her gaze to Tanner. Stopping short of throwing herself into his arms, she hugged him, never wanting to let him go. "You stay safe, too," she said aloud.

As her expert training fought basic need and desire,

winning by a hair, the warrior in her took over and she eased away from his chest. He'd be okay. He had to be, she wasn't about to lose another man she loved.

Port grabbed the duffle, all the time keeping pace at Tanner's side, and they ran for the parking area. Solace conjured wings and leapt into the night sky tracking Bliss. Locating her vibe off to the right, she soared in that direction. The wings she'd chosen were made for speed—no need now for heavy battle gear.

Solace spotted Bliss. Zooming in closer, she flew rings around her sister, tossing out faerie dust with each pass to get her attention. You didn't just casually approach a pair of iron tipped combat wings at full throttle and tap the owner on the shoulder.

Bliss pulled up short and hovered. Solace eased over and did the same.

"Mother found their lair."

"Is it over there?" Bliss asked, pointing to the exact bearing.

"Yes, but…"

"I feel a great amount of fear coming from there." Bliss shuddered. "Guess that's why I didn't lock in on your approach."

Solace remained silent, still hovering at the slowest possible revs. She couldn't feel fear, Bliss' specialty, but she could feel negative energy, and there was a cosmic bucket-load of it coming from that direction, also.

"Let's go." She nodded toward Bliss. "I'm tethered to Port. She's this way."

Side by side, they looped around trying to locate 55th Street. Then they spotted Tanner's truck as it raced through the night toward the Reps' hideout. Slowing down, they flew above the treetops and followed his vehicle to the property.

As he jagged onto a side road leading to the back of the house and the equestrian facility, Tanner cut his headlights. Good idea, she mentally agreed. A frontal attack would not have been her first choice either. Their minds were in sync as far as battle strategy.

When the truck rolled to a stop, she landed beside the driver's door and 86'd her wings. Tanner climbed out, and eyes wide stood staring at her. She glanced down. Her pretty, red dress, now split up the side, revealed her left leg to mid-thigh. And still in battle-mode, her tribal tattoos glowed softly in the light of a bright half-moon. They were both wired, their bodies flooded with adrenalin, anticipation, and the need to conquer the enemy. Stepping closer, he placed his hands on her shoulders and studied her face as if it might be his last opportunity.

"Too bad we're not heading for bed rather than bedlam," he said, with the crooked smile she'd come to love.

She captured his mouth with hers, letting him know she felt the same way. "My thoughts exactly," she whispered against his lips.

"We'll make up for it later," he reassured.

It was pre-battle banter, making plans for the future, even though if things went wrong, there might not be a future for either one of them.

"Come along children," Bliss interrupted. "Save the world first, play later."

Port started grabbing equipment out of the bed of the truck. She moved with deadly efficiency, readying for all-out war, which at the moment seemed pretty darn appropriate for what they were heading into. As they gathered around, she deployed the weapons.

Tanner exchanged his tux jacket for the camo one from behind the seat and settled a matching baseball cap on his head. Tightening the belt of the holstered Jericho 941 around his waist, he slung the strap of a small RPG-7 over his left shoulder and stuffed a few extra grenades in his pockets.

"Perfect for "shoot-and-scoot," he said.

"This will also drop a Rep in its tracks, or at least severely slow one down," Port said, pressing a .50 caliber Beowulf into his hands. It was one step up from an AK47.

"Holly hell. You guys really did come loaded for bear. This is turning out to be my kind of evening out after all." Tanner looked pleased, and ready for anything.

Solace hoped they all were. Facing Reps, you never knew what might happen.

Still dressed in black leather, Port checked and holstered her particle laser and uncased her favorite two-handed sword—Medieval gone twenty-first century Goth.

Like a Tombstone gunslinger, Bliss wore two laser pistols, one on each hip. She too appeared formidable.

"Grab that ammo box," Port instructed Solace. "You can be the first to use the new Zaradust laser grenades."

"But you love weaponry, Port. And these are just in from the outer realms. I thought you'd want the honor."

"Tonight I'm up for some hands on entertainment," Port countered, adjusting the double-edged sword in the harness across her back. "Nothing can compare to personally lopping off an enemy's head."

Nobody had to ask her twice, Solace did as instructed.

They deployed forward to evaluate the indoor arena and assess the number of enemy. Every light in the building burned bright, and she heard music playing. The friggin' Reps were partying.

Flattened up against the building, the team moved sideways along the north wall until they reached a row of high narrow windows. Closest to the first one, Solace eased sideways enough to peek in the bottom corner of plexi-glass. At her side, Tanner did the same.

"Holy mother," he whispered. "Each time I see one of those ugly brutes, they look bigger."

"The harder they fall," she whispered back.

All the Reps within view were carousing and having a good old time. All except one. This Rep stood off to the side, a big cigar clamped between his scaly lips, a drink clutched in one clawed hand. He seemed somehow removed from the general commotion echoing around the sand-filled room. It had to be Smith in Rep-form, holding himself above the other peons. Even among the Reps, there were class distinctions.

Shifting her gaze, she studied the huge domed structure in more detail. The owners must have trained or boarded a large number of horses here. They'd never believe what their new renters were doing in the place. One of the Reps stopped cavorting long enough to rip a chunk of meat off a fresh deer carcass hanging from a rough-hewn crossbeam. It made her want to puke as he stuffed the raw meat in his mouth, blood running down his chin. They were good at hunting, she'd give them that, and poaching laws would be the least of their worries.

The Rep she'd labeled as Smith, sauntered over to one of the stalls. He eased open the top half of the Dutch-door and looked in. A high-pitched screaming ensued. It had to be the models. At least some of them sounded alive. Smith laughed, deep and lusty. Wanting in on the fun, two other Reps dared to draw closer. When Smith snarled, they backed off. "I get first pick," he growled.

*You'll get no pick, Mr. Smith, if I have anything to say about it.*

Solace and Tanner pulled back. The others huddled closer, and they regrouped.

"How many, Solace?" Port asked.

"I saw six, including Smith."

"And you, Tanner?" Port questioned.

He nodded, appearing a little surprised to be asked. "Affirmative. Six. Do we have a plan this time?" A little bit of sarcasm flavored his words.

Port spoke first, of course. "I say Solace blasts a hole in the big sliding doors, we all go through together, then we take them out however we prefer. It's hard to choreograph hand to hand combat."

"I agree with Port." Solace nodded. "But Bliss should try to reach the women. She can calm them down enough to follow directions should we have to make a run for it."

"Works for me," Tanner agreed. "But with four of us in there, remember to keep tabs on each other's position. No friendly fire mishaps."

Low to the ground, they scrambled sideways past the windows then stood facing the main doors.

"There's a lot of hay in there," Solace pointed out.

"Let's try not to set it on fire. At least not until we're sure there aren't any horses in there."

She dropped to the ground, set up the tripod, and rested the Zaradust grenade launcher on top. Clicking the devise on, she felt more than heard it as it powered up to full capacity. Her heart rate quickened. Just how much kick did this bad-boy generate? Only one way to find out. When the green light came on, she whispered the all-clear-ready warning and squeezed the trigger. Suffering minimal recoil, she watched as the doors disintegrated. No flying pieces-parts, no fuss no muss, and barely any dust—just a gaping hole.

Leaping up, she claimed second place as she tore through the opening right behind Tanner. Seeing him in action, she felt inspired. Never hesitating, he seemed all valor and muscle and unshakable confidence. What soldier wouldn't follow such a leader, even to the borders of hell?

He cut to the right, she faded left. The Reps froze, mouths gaping. But they recovered quickly. Already airborne, Port took full advantage of the arena, a perfect venue for flying. With a battle cry on her lips, she streaked by the nearest Rep, swinging the weapon she so cherished in a downward arc, relieving him of his head. Suddenly the arena seemed a lot smaller as a putrid smell rose up from his dead body.

Dropping the RPG, Tanner dug in his heels and swung the Beowulf into position, letting loose with a spate of bullets. The Reps scattered in all directions, one coming straight at Solace. A laser blast shot past her, hitting the enemy in the chest. Bliss gave her a grin and kept flying, heading toward the stall where the models were being held. The injured Rep stumbled to one side allowing Solace time to jag out of his way and blast him with her own particle laser, taking out his eyes. He lurched wildly and crashed into a wall. He wouldn't be any trouble for a while.

Smith came roaring across the arena, bullets not deterring him, sand spewing up behind as he headed for Tanner. Never flinching, Tanner held his ground, and at the very last moment, he used the lizard's forward momentum against him. He tucked and kicked up with both feet, rolling backward, flipping their enemy head over heels. Grabbing a loop of sturdy rope lying near where the slaughtered deer hung, he hogtied Smith like a Pro Rodeo Hall-of-Famer, taking Smith alive.

Solace tossed Tanner the RPG. Locking and loading on the run, he cut across the open space and launched a grenade at two Reps who made the mistake of advancing one in front of the other. Now they were both toast, but the hay she'd been worried about caught flack and burst into flame. As the fire crackled, the heat rose, but at least the smell of smoke helped to mask the stink of dead Reps.

One Rep's lizard brain kicked in, and he tried to flee the building, the terror bright in his eyes. Port cut him off and herded him into a corner. Solace flash moved over to Bliss' position. The three models were on their feet, looking scared but not hysterical. Bliss' soothing magic had done the trick.

Tanner reconned the perimeter, checking out the tack room and each stall. The Rep she'd wounded earlier made the mistake of getting up. The fight didn't last long.

Stopping a moment to catch her breath, Solace watched Port having it out with a Rep defending himself with a pitchfork. Then she noticed the flames were growing faster. Still mentally tethered, Solace warned Port the fire was sneaking up behind her.

Port signaled back, and having run out of "playtime", she got down to business sending the Rep to meet his doom. "Yahoo," she exclaimed as she landed beside Solace.

"Yahoo?"

"Well we are in a barn. Glad for their sake, but sad for mine, there aren't any horses here. I'd sure like to go for a ride. I'm so hyper I'll be up for hours."

"We haven't located the employee from NOAA," Solace said. "Searching for him should help you unwind."

"I don't think he's in here. None of us saw him while airborne," Port reported.

Tanner jogged over. "We gotta get out of here."

The howl of approaching fire engines screamed in the night, reinforcing his advice, and it sounded like a chopper circled overhead.

"But where's Smith?" she asked. "I saw you take him down, but I don't see a body."

"He's over….What the heck. He's gone. I had him subdued and tied."

"The gnarly puke probably chewed through the ropes," Port said.

Bliss joined them and rested a hand on Solace's arm. "The girls are heading for full blown shock. We need to get them to a hospital."

Solace glanced over to the three pale wide-eyed faces. "Okay. Tanner you take them in the truck. We'll try to track down Smith. And hopefully your NOAA employee."

Chapter Nineteen

Their search the previous night for Smith, the drone, and Andy, had been long, exhausting, and unrewarding. But thank goodness the models were safe, and other than probably having nightmares for the rest of their lives, they were okay. Once thoroughly debriefed, they would be strongly encouraged to have counseling or selective amnesia.

The three Faes, or The Winged Fury, as Bliss was calling the sisters today, stared at the hologram board floating just midway off the floor in their office. Most police agencies and special op units had a "murder" board to which they referred as they ferreted out clues needed to solve a case. The sisters had decided to call this one their "mother" board. After all, Mother had supplied it, and with direct access, she could look at and update the mystical contraption at will.

Solace glared at the photos of Smith. Catching a lucky break, they had his DNA from the cigar he'd been smoking in the barn, and they had images now of both his Hume and Rep form. He had mean eyes even for a lizard brain. But in Hume form, just like at the country club, he appeared downright handsome, no doubt a helpful attribute when enticing females to their doom.

They also had DNA evidence from the scene where each woman had been murdered. And although the local authorities couldn't find a match, they had. In five of the six scenes, it turned out to be Smith's. One of his compatriots evidently killed the other woman. The terrorized models had been unbelievably fortunate.

"Smith is going to be in one pissy mood after last night," Port said, sucking on a banana popsicle. She'd developed a fondness for them, occasionally even considering them a substitute for a real breakfast with a real banana.

"I agree." Bliss nodded. "And since we rescued his victims, I'm afraid he'll be on the prowl again soon."

Solace stepped up to the board. "At least we have the satisfaction of knowing we took out five members of his crew. Although," she said, tapping the board, "Smith and this one are still at large." Wielding a large red laser marker, she slashed the light across each of the Reps who no longer posed a problem, and highlighted the photo of their unknown adversary hovering beside Smith. "We're whittling down the enemy in this area. And we'll get that guy too." In the photo, the new Rep seemed to gaze back at her with mocking eyes and a sarcastic smile.

"No doubt they'll send replacements," Port put in, tossing her popsicle stick in the recycle bin.

"But they'll probably have to come from off-earth, and according to Mother they're behind on training. Plus the Big Pharma under their thumb is having trouble keeping up production of the transformation serum. They can't afford to have the lot of them running around looking like the monsters they are. At least not yet."

"I feel bad we never found Andy," Bliss said.

"It does bode ill. But we haven't located the drone

stolen from Peterson Air Force Base either. I think it leaves some hope Andy is still alive, and they need him to program the device."

"So what's on the docket for today?" Port asked.

"I called the office where Smith works," Solace said. "According to his secretary he didn't show up today. A Mr. Jones is taking his calls. After last night's debacle, I have a feeling Smith's going to dump the business scenario and start over with a new identity. We need to investigate this Jones fellow though. See if he's a Rep too, or just an innocent Hume." She studied the photo of the unknown subject wondering if that could be Jones.

"Speaking of Humes, what's Tanner up to today," Port asked. "He held his own at the barn."

"You really are starting to like him," Solace teased.

"Hard not to, I admit it."

"He's training all day. After last night, it's obvious we need to get more men up to speed. The Army immediately took over fighting the fire, and the Boulder County officials were ordered to stay clear of the area. That limited civilians getting a glimpse at the Reps. But because the recruits need to be aware of exactly what they're facing, he's taking them to the equestrian facility later. Nothing like firsthand experience."

Port gagged. "Hope they have gasmasks. The stench from there must have reached the Exosphere by now."

"I don't envy them," Solace agreed. "So, anybody up for a little stakeout activity. Anybody?"

"I'm meeting up with Nathaniel this morning," Bliss said, opting out. "They're still working on the parallel clock set up, so that areas restricted, but I can check out the rest of the facility—and him. We hardly had any time together last night. "

"Mother gave me permission for two hours at the stable." Port snagged Solace's cowboy hat and tried it on. Of course it fit perfectly. "I'm wired. If I don't burn off some of this energy, I refuse to be responsible for my actions. You know I can't sit still or think straight when I'm in hyper-drive."

"Probably would help if you ate something besides sugar for breakfast," Solace pointed out.

"A theory never to be tested." Port headed for the door. "I'll catch up with you as soon as I get back."

"I'm out of here, too," Bliss said, giving Solace a hug.

Solace hugged her back and watched her sisters leave.

Okay, so she'd do the stakeout on her own. No big deal, couldn't get into too much trouble just watching a building, no need for backup.

Rather than call, she left a text message for Tanner regarding her plan. She knew prior to taking the recruits to see the ranch where the Reps had stayed, the men would be practicing water rescue and underwater demo. Tanner might be underwater right now.

As she headed for her car, a smile snuck up on her—it seemed to happen a lot when she thought of Tanner. She knew his leaving active duty with the Rangers just about broke his heart, but he seemed to be warming up to the idea of teaching a new team, one vital to security. And from what she saw, he appeared to be good at his job. He'd quickly won the respect of his men. No doubt his reputation preceded him.

He'd run a bucket load of missions, not all of them

covert, which explained how his body got broken in parts. Heat coiled around her. As far as she was concerned, the parts which counted worked better than all right. He seemed to smile more, too. She liked to think she had something to do with that phenomenon. And although losing a man weighed heavily on him, it also made him even more determined to train harder and fight smarter. New enemies required new tactics and new strategies.

****

Missing the bulk of the commuter traffic, Solace reached downtown Boulder more quickly than expected. The business district laid claim to a few "skyscrapers", severely limited in height by the rampant environmental groups, and Mr. Smith's office lurked among them. Parking her hybrid near a food wagon, she scrunched down in the seat and punched on her cell phone. Again the secretary answered her call, reconfirming the previous information about Smith not being available with calls being taken by Mr. Jones. She begged off, stating she would call back later.

****

As he toured the office, Mr. Jones fought not to laugh out loud. It belonged to him now. The Mercedes in the underground garage, the corporate bank account—everything.

Smith had gone MIA, unreachable and hopefully dead, although Intel reported his body hadn't been found at the equestrian ranch. Since his old rival knew all the tricks, the possibility of his being alive couldn't be discounted. Either way, it spelled the end for Smith. He'd screwed up royally.

When the intercom on the desk buzzed, Jones

nearly jumped out of his human form. Then he reached over and clicked the speaker on.

"Yes, Veronica."

"Call for you on line two, Mr. Jones."

"Who is it?"

"They refused to leave a name, sir."

"Man or woman?"

"A gentleman. He asked specifically for you, not for Mr. Smith."

"Put him through please." Not hard to guess who this would be.

"Enjoying the view, Jones?"

"Yes, as a matter of fact I am. Where are you, Smith?"

"Somewhere safe."

"Heard about your little barn dance. Sounds like quite the hot mess."

"The U.S. Army's been brought in," Smith defended.

"Yes. I know. A special team, just for fighting us. That's old news. What do you want?"

"I want to make a deal."

"Why should I? Besides, you're rather out of bargaining chips"

"I still have the drone. A prize, which if used correctly, could put your career over the top."

The drone...their commander really would take notice if he had such a big ticket item in his pocket. "What do you want in exchange?"

"You've got friends in the Documents Department, and you're an off-planet liaison. I need papers and a ticket out of here. And serum, plenty of serum."

"Yes, I'm afraid you are expendable now aren't

you? The Humes and Fae know what you look like, and your sexual predilections haven't won you any friends either. I told you to be more discreet, to wait longer between "feedings". You never were any good at self-control."

Like music to his ears, the ensuing silence brought Jones to muted laughter. He visualized Smith seething at having to humble himself, admitting defeat and asking for help.

"Just worry about your own obsessions, they're no less dangerous. Do you want the drone or not?" Smith growled.

"Yes, it's a deal. Does it come with the employee from NOAA? Not much good without a programmer."

"Of course. He's a little worse for wear. The Earth nerd is surprisingly stubborn and patriotic, but with encouragement he'll do. He's already made modifications for us."

"Where and when."

"Take Sunshine Canyon Drive west toward the foothills. There's a turn-off just past Green Rock road. We can meet there."

"How will I find you?"

"Bring a communicator. I still have mine."

"I'll see you in about half an hour, with the paperwork," he lied.

"Not a problem. Don't forget the serum."

He had no intention of helping his old nemesis. Surely Smith had considered such a possibility, but then he supposed desperate men made desperate decisions. And why did he need so much serum? A sudden chill crept though him, frigid enough to disturb even his cold blood. What could Smith really be up to?

\*\*\*\*

The face of the man exiting the office building, matched the photo Solace had laid out on the dash in front of her. He was their unidentified subject, their unknown Rep in human form. But was he Mr. Jones?

Hitting redial for the office, the secretary informed her she just missed Mr. Jones who was leaving the building as they spoke. Gotcha now buddy. Scrunching down farther in the seat of her car, she watched the man walk to the underground parking. Two minutes later, driving a Mercedes, he barreled out of the covered lot and onto the street. It appeared to be the same car they had tagged as Smith's—didn't even let the engine cool did you Mr. Jones?

She followed at a safe distance, and using hands-free, left messages for Tanner and Port, asking Port to relay the info to Bliss. There seemed little choice but to tail Jones.

Even in human form, the Rep drove like the demon he was, and her little hybrid struggled to keep up. Wherever he was going, he seemed in a great hurry to get there. Heading west out of town and deeper into the foothills, she wondered if her cell reception would hold out if and when anyone got back to her. Her particle laser, fully charged, lay on the passenger seat. She tossed the photo of Jones beside it. Not to worry. She could handle whatever this joker threw at her.

He turned off into a visitor center parking area. Thank goodness only one other car occupied the lot. Civilian interference or interaction always complicated things. She braked to a stop. A thick stand of pine lining the entryway sheltered her gently purring car from his view.

Through the boughs she watched Jones exit his vehicle. He glanced around and then spoke into what appeared to be some type of communication device. Slipping the unit into his jacket pocket, he reached through the open car window and grabbed a large envelope. With another quick look around, he headed into the woods.

Maneuvering the car closer, she cut the engine, slid from the vehicle, and shed her blazer. Something told her she might need quick access to her wings. Gently closing the car door, and with laser in hand, she followed. The uneven terrain and low hanging branches made approaching quietly difficult, still she got as close as she dared. As the trees thinned into a small open valley, Jones stopped and so did she.

"I'm here, Smith. Where are you? I don't have time for games," he called.

"Did you bring the passport and serum?"

"Sure, buddy. It's all right here." Jones set a large padded envelope on the ground then stepped back several paces.

Smith emerged from the nearby trees in Rep form. Jones showed no emotional reaction, but he slid his right hand inside his jacket as if going for a weapon. Quietly, she clicked the safety off her laser.

Smith retrieved the envelope and clawed it open. Then he roared and tossed it aside. "You backstabbing traitor." He lumbered forward, limping badly. When he raised a fist in anger, scales fell from his arm. He appeared to be deteriorating. Could it be from lack of serum? Or did changing back and forth at will eventually have a toxic effect?

"You look like hell Smith," Jones taunted.

"Don't laugh too hard. You were changed only a few months after me, and with prolonged use, the serum appears to have a few nasty side effects. Soon you'll need more and more. And I'm beginning to think, at some point, even that won't help."

Jones remained silent as if contemplating the full meaning of Smith's information. "I haven't heard anything about this," he scoffed.

"Of course not. If word got out, the higher ups would have a panic on their hands. They think of us as disposable. Always another Reptile soldier to take your place. But if the new recruits discover changing is fatal, there won't be many of them signing up for Earth duty."

"In that case," Jones said, oh so pleasantly, "sounds like you're as good as dead. So where's the drone?"

The words stepped up her heart rate. If the drone was here, it followed Andy would be. too. She needed backup. Summoning her sisters crossed her mind, but some Reps were known to pick up on telepathy. Too bad she wasn't still tethered to Port. Best to lay low—at least right now.

For a galactic second, Smith appeared confused. Maybe his brain had begun deteriorating along with his body. Then a frightful grin spread across his ugly face. Even for a Rep, he appeared demented. Turning, he made for an RV she'd noticed hidden in the trees off to the side of the valley. Jones pulled out a Ruger 9mm, and got one shot off. It went wide, and Smith gained the camper before Jones could fire again.

Figuring Jones would pursue Smith, Solace eased forward to take stock of the situation. But the remaining Rep seemed to catch wind of something. He turned abruptly, retracing his steps, and in the process spotted her.

Frick... Materializing wings, she shot straight up into the air, tree branches slapping at her as she headed for open airspace.

Taken by surprise, it took Jones a moment to realize the situation before he raised his pistol and fired. She flitted to the side and sent a laser blast his way. Her cover now blown, she summoned Bliss and Port with all her might.

What she heard next made her blue blood run cold.

Chapter Twenty

The Condor drone seemed to come out of nowhere.

Praying she wasn't the target, Solace crash-landed in the top of a sturdy fir tree. The drone strafed the ground near Jones. She couldn't tell if he'd been wounded as he scrambled to find cover. At least it hadn't come for her. She breathed a sigh of relief. But the feeling died a quick death. From her vantage point, she spotted trouble of another kind.

A school bus full of waving arms and muffled laughter entered the turnoff where she'd parked her car. A nice day for an outing, unless a heat seeking missile blew your picnic table to the outskirts of Hade.

Seeing no other choice, she pushed off from the tree, not thinking twice about leaving its protection as she circled to the right and glided over toward where the school bus would most likely park. Feet barely touching the ground, she scrapped her wings and set down behind a large juniper, her forward momentum giving her an extra push as she sprinted forward. Her top Clearance I.D. out of her back pocket and in her hand, she met the yellow behemoth just as it rolled to a stop and the bi-fold doors snapped opened.

"I'm sorry," she hollered over the hum of excited children's voice. "You need to return to your school, or pick a different park. This one is off limits today."

"What are you talking about?" the driver

demanded. "Who are you?"

"I'll handle this, Charlie." The woman's comment silenced the man behind the wheel. She stepped down to stand before Solace, the playful chaos in the bus spilling down the steps behind her. "I'm Miss Archer, their teacher. Why should we leave? What's going on?" The woman raised her voice trying to be heard over the shrieks and laughter.

Other than the truth, what could Solace tell her? Claiming a bear sighting or an escaped fugitive would scare the kids too much. Why not blame it on Mother Nature? That idea appealed to her. "There's a dam over the ridge behind me," Solace began. "We detected an area that appears weakened from last year's flash flood. Nothing to be overly concerned about, but in the off chance it gives way, anyone in this area would be swept down the valley."

"You're lying. I've been here several times. There's no dam up there."

"It would be best for you to take me at my word," Solace advised, wangling her I.D. in hopes of gaining her attention.

With a smile, she captured the woman's gaze and held it. Although rarely used, the Fae gift to compel might be her only hope. However, the gift came with great responsibility and had limitations. If wielded for evil or malice, the user would pay a price. But in this case, with the greater good at stake, it seemed a safe choice.

Blocking out visions of Reps and drones, Solace focused her concentration. Just a little more internal tinkering. There, that should do it.

Now the teacher smiled as well. "Yes, you're right

of course," she apologized. "What was I thinking? Thank you for making us aware of the danger." Climbing back onboard the bus, she spoke briefly to the driver, and the doors slapped shut.

Assured they were on their way out, Solace sneaked down the hill on foot, crossing the tree-studded south side of the valley. At the edge, shielded by the groundcover, she scoped out the area. Deciding to pull out all the stops and use every survival tool in her arsenal, she revved up her hypervision.

Even for short periods of time, this Fae power required tremendous energy. Clicking off, she decided the time and effort had been well spent. Her heat detecting capabilities let her know two bodies were near the RV—one very large, one normal. Another heat source registered in the little rustic bathroom facility. Probably Jones hiding out for a while. Who could blame him? At least she assumed Jones' body heat caused the blip on her visual radar. Other than small animals, she saw no indications of living beings within a hundred yard radius.

The urge to chase down Jones simmered in her veins, but rescuing Andy came first. Besides, with the Condor waiting for another chance at Jones, he wouldn't be going anywhere soon. First things first.

Weaving between tree trunks and stepping over fallen logs, she headed for the camper. Then ten yards of open space brought her up short. She had to take the chance. Deep breath in, she flash-moved forward. Back pressed against the hot metal of the RV, she exhaled and waited to see if she'd been discovered. Laser at the ready, she heard two voices. One sounded like the gruff voice of a Rep, and the other had to be the terrified voice of Andy.

"Do it," Smith growled.

"I'm trying," Andy babbled. "You said your kind has different blood. It's not even red for pity's sake. Considering these discrepancies, I can't be sure the heat seeking properties are working correctly. I told you, I don't program drones for a living, it's just a hobby."

"And I told you what will happen to your family if you don't obey me. Do it," Smith bellowed.

His voice boomed so loudly, Solace swore the nearby trees quivered.

"God forgive me," Andy cried.

The sound of the drone taking off startled her, and she instinctively cringed as it came screaming over the top of the RV, right over her position. But her luck held, and it kept going, heading in the direction of the log-built bathrooms.

Still experimental but apparently working just dandy, the Condor carried two hundred rounds of ammunition, and two heat seeking missiles. At the sound of an explosion, which really did shake the earth, she figured one of the HSMs had found its target. Gaining higher ground, she spied a pile of flaming rubble where the rustic log bathroom had once stood. Was Jones still inside?

As Andy brought the drone back home for a landing, she hurried to the other side of the RV.

"Nice work Andy. The world's a better place with one less Rep in it."

Smith lumbered around to face her, his lizard eyes wide with surprise.

She kept her laser trained square on his chest. Shooting him would have been a pleasure, but getting information from him trumped the urge.

"You're next," the Rep promised. "But not with this," he sneered, snatching the handheld control box and monitor from Andy's grasp. "I want to personally kill and eat you. Maybe I'll start the eating before the killing." As if he could already taste her, spittle dangled from one side of his mouth. He raised the equipment as if to smash it on the ground.

"No," Andy screamed, jumping up and down, trying to reach the equipment.

"It's okay, Andy. I can take care of myself. I need you to run to the parking lot as fast as you can. Take my car and leave."

"It's not okay. You don't understand. The Condor has a failsafe. If you smash the controls, it will seek out the nearest forms not imprinted as friendly. He and I are in the data base, you're not."

Smith seemed to be considering this information. He stared at her, then at the box, then back at her. When a finger dropped off his left hand, he snarled and spit out a vivid curse in Rep language. "Always did enjoy a good air show," he wheezed, breathing hard.

Throwing down the control panel, he stomp it flat with one scaly foot and ground it into the dirt. His booming laughter echoed down the little valley until a coughing spell cut the outburst short.

"Run and hide," Andy shrieked, as the drone came alive. Finally taking his own advice, he scrambled into the woods.

Conjuring a set of wings built for speed, Solace headed for the heavens. She could fly to a height beyond the Condor's capability, but the thought of leaving a rogue drone to its own devices didn't sit well with her. Could she create a whirlwind strong enough to put it out of commission? She better hope so, because here it came.

Pointing her toes like a ballerina, she raised her arms and chanted to the powers of the East. Spinning faster and faster, her tattoos glowed, and the boughs on nearby trees lashed back and forth. Dust rose up from the dirt road far below.

Although wobbling and tumbling in the turbulence, the drone managed to fire its second heat seeking missile. She tucked and rolled and dived toward the still burning visitors' restroom. Holding her breath, she flew right through the flames, singeing her wings and the tips of her hair.

The missile hit the last standing log wall, blasting it to smithereens. She gained altitude, a smile tugging at her lips. Unlike a quadrotor or a quadcopter, the Condor UAV mimicked a standard airplane in design, and it had just fired its last heat seeker. But the undeterred high-tech piece of equipment wasn't done yet. She felt a dogfight coming on. This could prove to be fun.

Laser safety off, she circled around, cutting altitude to tail the drone. Part of her Earth History classes had included the combat strategy of WWI and WWII. She had studied every video she could get her hands on, especially those of the Red Baron, watching them over and over and over, until she knew each thrilling move by heart. *Kick the tires, and light the fires*, she was going in.

Detecting her presence, the Condor took evasive action. Programed to position the sun at its back to compromise her vision, the drone jinked high, but not so wide. *Not gonna fall for that old trick, you flying droid.* Pulling a boom and zoom, she lasered the Condor's left wing before plunging to near ground level. The drone fought to maintain equilibrium, quickly recovering.

Flying backward, Solace cursed. The stupid thing just wouldn't die. It barrel rolled, almost as if showing off, before sending bullets flying and heading straight for her. With a quick turn, she again sought shelter in the top of a cluster of dense pines. A broken branch, which she saw too late, cut into her arm. Blue blood ran from shoulder to wrist, but the bullets slamming into the limbs and tree trunks took her mind off the pain.

Keeping her target in sight, she shot straight up into the air. The drone, not built or programed for confronting a Fae, veered off to make another sweep. Now she had the edge, and she blasted away, achieving a direct hit. The drone shuddered and sputtered, spiraling out of control. With a last ditch effort, it let loose a parting salvo. One bullet tore through her right wing. It stung like the devil, and as the hole ripped bigger, maintaining altitude got dicey.

Plummeting like a rock, the Condor crashed and burned, giving off surprisingly little fire, but plenty of smoke. Solace held her position, trying to get her bearings as she relaxed her body and willed her pulse and breathing rate to drop. When she got back to the apartment, she wanted a big honking margarita, or better still a Slow Macros Fizz like the ones they made on Macros 5.

She glanced down at her surroundings, and a truck careening into the parking lot grabbed her attention. It bounced over the cement parking dividers and across the picnic area, briefly slowing at the smoldering restroom. Then gaining speed, it skidded into a left turn and headed for the still smoking drone.

As she treaded air, her heartbeat speeded up again—it was Tanner. Dang…she must look a mess. Laser in one hand, she used the other to smooth back her hair. Why did it feel wet? And why did her head suddenly hurt like blue blazes? She touched her scalp again, studied her hand, and reared back in wonder. Where had all this blood come from? Flush with battle-courage, she hadn't felt the head wound—until now. Pain shot through her brain like a steel-tipped arrow, keeping up a tortured rhythm with the pulse pounding in both ears.

She closed her eyes and concentrated on keeping her wings moving just enough to stay airborne. Now she felt woozy. Could you get a concussion while in the air?

The hole in her right wing ripped another two inches. She air staggered to one side trying to level out as she lowered altitude. *Too high.* The words kept crossing her mind as woozy turned to fading fast.

Locking her wings into auto-glide, she passed out.

Chapter Twenty-One

Down shifting, and with the truck's tires spinning, Tanner left the smoking rubble of the visitors' restrooms behind. Then bouncing off rocks and over ruts, he zigzagged between the trees. *Where was she? Where was she?* The words pounded through his head like a litany as he skidded into a turn and headed in a different direction.

When he'd read her text, and then couldn't find her at Smith's office in Boulder, he'd gotten the distinct feeling she could use some help. She shouldn't have gone off on her own to begin with, but he supposed her independent nature and do-or-die call to duty were traits he'd better grow accustomed to.

Her car was in the parking lot, she had to be here somewhere. Thankfully, she'd left her GPS emergency signal on or he wouldn't have found her car. At the edge of a valley, he cut the engine and rolled to a stop. The RV off to the right didn't show any signs of life. About twenty yards straight ahead, another pile of rubble smoked, this one much smaller than the burned-out john. Wanting to explore on foot, he reached for the door handle, but someone blocked his efforts to push open the door.

"Thank God. You have to help us." The hysterical man reached through the open window grasping at Tanner's shirt.

Tanner forced the truck door open, maneuvering the person out of the way. "Calm down," he ordered. On closer inspection, he recognized Andy. "It's okay Andy. You're safe now."

Andy collapsed against the hood of the truck, one hand clutching at his chest, his breath coming in gasps.

"Do you recognize me, Andy?" Tanner asked, trying to assess the man's lucidness.

"Yes. You're Tanner Jackson. We both work at NOAA. They made me do it," he added, as the expression of terror returned to his eyes."

"Who made you do what?"

"The...the monsters. I tried to get away. I tried to destroy the drone. Then some woman showed up. She saved me."

A woman. It had to be Solace. "Where is she, Andy?"

"I don't know. She told me to run...I was so confused, I didn't get far."

"Think, man," he ordered, taking a step closer. "Where did you last see her?"

"I don't know. I don't know."

Tamping down his frustration, Tanner tilted back his head and blew out a heavy breath. That's when he saw her. Still not accustomed to her many unusual capabilities, he'd forgotten to search for her airborne.

The tension in his shoulders and gut eased. He waved, but the lack of response sent his stomach back on alert. Something must be wrong. Her wings appeared ridged and set, not flapping or fluttering—and one of them sported a jagged tear. Gliding in lazy circles, she spiraled closer and closer to the ground. He could see her face now. Eyes closed, head tipped to the side, bright blue blood marked one cheek and the front of her clothing.

*Please God*, he prayed, *don't let her be dead.*

Another two spirals and she came within reach. Arms outstretched, he snatched her from the air, preventing her from crashing to the earth. Gathering her body close, all the while trying to avoid her wings, he held her tightly, kissing her full on the mouth as if trying to awaken a sleeping beauty.

"Solace," he called, giving her a gentle shake. Her wings hung limp, nearly touching the ground. Why didn't she come around? "Open your eyes. Can you hear me?" The blood she wore seemed mostly dried, no active bleeding. A small relief, but better than nothing.

Heading toward the truck, it looked as if he'd have to put her in the bed. With her wings extended, she'd never fit in the seat. The idea did not sit well with him. Thankfully, she moaned and opened her eyes, rendering the point moot.

"Hi darlin', everything's going to be okay. Sorry I couldn't get here sooner."

"You got here just in time," she said, nestling her head against his shoulder.

After a moment she stiffened in his arms and glanced around. "I have to go back. I think Jones died when they bombed the restroom, but Smith is still alive over by the RV."

"You'll do no such thing." He tightened his grip as she squirmed for freedom. "And that's an order, which you have to obey because I've been promoted to Captain. After you're safe and I get a good look at your wounds, I'll go check it out. By the way, you have a big hole in one wing."

"My wings? I forgot. Guess I *am* a little out of it."

As he opened his mouth to ask if they hurt, and if she could make them disappear, they turned into mist. "Is mindreading also one of your skills?" he asked, with a shake of his head. "I was just about to ask you to 86 the aviation gear."

"No, I can't read your mind," she reassured with a grin, "so your secrets are safe. But I noticed Andy over by your truck, and I didn't want to freak him out any more than he already is. Poor guy. They threatened to harm his family if he didn't cooperate."

"Did he see you all *faerie-fied*?"

"Once, but he was hysterical. He may have already forgotten about it."

"Okay. Let's just worry about you. Besides, if he saw a Rep in full regalia, he's probably either ready to accept anything, or ready to deny all."

"Hey, Andy," he called, as they headed toward the truck. "Get the door, will ya buddy."

At the sound of Tanner's voice, Andy jumped. Then as if coming to his senses, he obliged, and Tanner gently eased Solace onto the passenger seat. She gave a whimper but never said a word.

Leaning in, he smoothed her hair back to check the wound on her head. A large bump had formed beneath the nasty cut. Although no longer bleeding, it had been—profusely. And it appeared to be the cause of the blood staining the front of her clothing.

Straightening, he stood beside the truck and keyed in the Army Search and Rescue Team's number on his cell phone. After the Army had gotten wind of the underground war between the Faes and Reps, they not only created the undercover fighting unit which he commanded, they demanded to be more instrumental in running the show. Since the Army was risking some of their own men, Mother allowed limited information and participation. On the up side, the Army organized a special Search and Rescue Team, a medical unit reserved only for soldiers and casualties related to the covert op. Schooled in Fae anatomy and physiology, he felt safe allowing them to check Solace out and deciding if she needed further treatment.

"Andy," he said loudly, shoving the cell phone back in his pocket. The man looked to be heading for shock again.

"What's wrong? Are they coming back to get us?"

"You're safe, Andy," Tanner reassured again. "Get hold of yourself. I need you to sit in the driver's seat of the truck and lock the doors. Stay with Solace. Protect Solace." The last idea being more a case of *Solace will protect you.*

"I couldn't possibly drive," Andy said, wringing his hands.

No kidding. The last place this shell-shocked guy should be was behind the wheel of a vehicle on the road.

"I'm not asking you to." Tanner patted the truck keys nestled in his other pocket. Wouldn't want Andy suddenly going rogue and really trying to rescue Solace. "Get in," he repeated, bodily assisting Andy into the truck. "Lock the doors and stay put. Paramedics are on the way."

He waited until Andy followed his instructions then headed for the RV.

Ten feet from the camper, a wave of noxious odors washed over him. It smelled like death. Gun in hand, he edged around to the back. Smith sat on the ground, leaning up against a tree. He looked like hell, and that's just where Tanner yearned to send his scaly butt. Green blood oozed from open wounds, most of the fingers on his left hand were missing, and one eye leaked fluid.

Tanner masked his nose and mouth in the crook of his arm, trying to block the stench.

"Shoot me," Smith growled, shaking with pain.

As Tanner watched, the Rep lost an ear and a set of small crusty fins cracked and fell off the back of his neck. The "monster" didn't look so scary now. Hard to believe this rotting piece of debris had been responsible for not only kidnapping Andy and the models, but of cruelly assaulting those innocent women and brutally ending their lives. And now, because of this stinking SOB, Solace sat huddled and wounded in his truck. He lowered his arm from his face.

"Shoot me," Smith said again. His tail split open near the tip oozing something even more disgusting than green blood.

Tanner's finger itched to squeeze the trigger, but his orders had been to take Smith alive

"That's why the Humes won't win this war," Smith taunted, with a half-paralyzed sneer. "Your compassion will be your undoing."

"Time will tell," he said evenly.

He wouldn't be baited into defending the characteristics which differentiated humans from this lowlife mutated lizard. On the other hand, it didn't appear Smith would live long enough to be properly question, or in fact, questioned at all. Killing him would actually *be* the humane thing to do.

"Come to think of it," he said, retraining his pistol

on the Rep. "Guess I'd do as much for any wounded animal."

"I'm not an animal, you puny human asshole." Smith snarled, reaching for his weapon.

Tanner pulled the trigger.

Chapter Twenty-Two

Tanner rested at Solace's back, and as the stillness of morning surrounding them in calm, he listened to her gentle breathing. Thank God, she hadn't been hurt as seriously as he first thought.

Refusing to let her out of his sight, when the Paramedics arrived, he'd insisted on riding with her in the ambulance to the Fae Clinic. He'd stayed by her side as they sutured her head wound and kept watch all night as the odd looking blue blood drip into her, finally bringing the color back to her cheeks.

They intended to monitor her all the next day for complications but gave in and discharged her as she prepared to stubbornly walk out without permission. Last night her sisters had treated her with their own brand of folk medicine and salves, and he'd held her while she slept.

This morning he wanted more than to just hold her, but what if it was too much too soon. Besides, if he had anything to say about it, they would have a lifetime of chances to make love. That being said, he couldn't resist touching her, offering her the choice.

****

Feigning sleep, Solace sighed with contentment while Tanner traced little patterns on her shoulder and around her wing ports. Then that same hand eased lower, to the curve of her hip, coming to rest on her bottom. A smile tugged at her lips, but she didn't open her eyes.

Safe and happy in her bed, she indulged in a moment of pure selfish lazitude—that is lazy with attitude. It sounded like a good plan until Tanner pressed a kiss to the nape of her neck, and his magic hand slipped around her waist and drew her naked body solidly up against his.

Her mood quickly went from lazy to full alert.

"You awake, darlin'?"

"Mmmm," she murmured.

It felt good to be alive. Good to know they had taken down Smith and Jones and made a dent in the Rep organization. Good to have someone in her life who made her feel this beautiful.

Stretching luxuriously, she bumped her backside against the part of him waiting for her personal attention, and the hand around her waist slipped lower, fingers coaxing and exciting until she could no longer pretend indifference. Twisting around to face him, she sought his mouth, offering deep kisses as she stroked and teased him in return.

"I've been so worried about you," he managed, between groans of pleasure. "You shouldn't have gone off by yourself."

"Nice to know you care," she joked.

She could have promised to never to do it again, but it would be a lie, and she never wanted to lie to Tanner. Trying to get his mind off the subject, she pressed her naked breasts against his naked chest. The tactic worked. He nuzzled her neck and eased her onto her back. She enjoyed it when he took the lead, acting as if he couldn't wait to get at her, to take her along with him to their special place. The weight of his body on hers felt comforting, almost sheltering, not controlling or threatening, and opening up to him, she let him have his way.

Levering up on his elbows, he rose up for a moment to gaze down at her. "Are you sure you're up for this? Fighting drones and taking down bad guys can be pretty brutal. I don't want to hurt you."

"Well, maybe we'd better stop."

He made a strangled sound, the expression on his face screaming *I don't want to, but I will.*

With a huge smile, she wrapped one leg around his thighs. "I'm kidding, of course. You're the best medicine a Fae female could want."

Permission granted and still watching her face, he slid into her, slowly so slowly. A breathy moan escaped her, and she leaned her head back and rocked against him. Taking her at her word, he quit playing nice, his beautiful body working hers, drawing out responses she longed for, sending her mind beyond her body on a transcendental cosmic holiday. The more time they spent together, the more intense the lovemaking. On the outside, her tattoos glowed, on the inside she turned to liquid heat ready to explode, ready to set her world on fire, and his too.

Framing his face with her hands, she watched the passion in his eyes darken and deepen. Her warrior proved as untiring in bed as on the battlefield. Fingernails gently raking, she glided her hands across his shoulders and downward. Despite the scars, his body couldn't be more beautifully formed. Her personal Adonis, whom she swore to keep safe, and not share with anyone, not even Aphrodite.

For a glorious moment, there was no time or space other than the here and now. Only Tanner wanting and needing her. Only her body responding to his, and her mind gone delirious with the way he made her feel.

"Can't wait much longer," he groaned.

"Then don't," she gasped.

Her words meshed into a scream of pleasure as a shuddering orgasm wiped out everything around her. She gripped his backside, and thrust upward. He drove deeper, following her over the cliff, sending a second wave of paradise washing over her. She trusted him enough to let go completely, and she thought he felt the same.

As breathing slowed and blood cooled, they remained locked in each other's arms. A Fae and a Hume, different species, different cultures, but now of one mind and one heart.

Tanner eased over to lie at her side, his left hand remaining on her abdomen, rising and falling with each breath she took. Covering his hand with hers, she intertwined their fingers.

Although happy and contented, she couldn't deny she felt bruised and battered. A session in the hot tub and some food sounded good. Her stomach growled like a Morovian bearcat—maybe food first.

When she made to rise, Tanner held her back. "Not yet," he coaxed. "You're so soft and warm. I love holding you." His arms drew her closer, and she reveled in the feeling of comfort.

"I love being held."

Her senses quickened, but not for round two. She felt the close presence of Port and Bliss. She also detected a weird sound she couldn't identify. A scratching noise, like claws on wood?

"Someone's outside the bedroom door," she whispered.

"You guys decent?" Port called.

She recaptured Tanner's hand and stilled his playful seduction. If he kept that up, they surely wouldn't be. "Should we let them in?" she whispered. He gave her that crooked grin and nodded yes.

"Okay, safe to come in," she called, drawing the sheet up over their bodies.

The door burst open, but neither Bliss nor Port were the first through the opening. A bizarre animal, looking like a bad science experiment, ran forward and loped around the room.

"What in the name of glory..." Tanner reached for his Jericho.

"Don't shoot. It's a Rapran."

"A Rapa-what. It's not part Reptile is it?"

"No way," they said in unison.

"I've photographed animals all around the world, but I've never seen anything even close to this mongrel. It looks half mastiff and half Bengal tiger. With maybe a little kangaroo thrown in based on the way it keeps jumping around."

"Zowns, it's huge," Solace said, sitting up uninhibited by her nakedness. Only having seen Raprans in pictures, its size came as a surprise. They'd been banished during the Transition years. At one time, they'd been experimented on by Out-worlders, making them vicious and uncontrollable. When Mother found out, she'd taken them all to a healing planet, and now, after generations of breeding for gentleness and loyalty, they were slowly being reintroduced as Fae companions.

"Good news/bad news," Port said.

"The Rapran is the good news," Bliss said, beaming at the creature. Then with one semi-stern glance, she had the Rapran come to heel.

Tanner had the covers nearly pulled up to his chin as he eyed the unusual beast.

"Their true name is Rapacious Ranivorous," Solace explained. "You can see why we call them Raprans. They eat frogs, and big or large reptiles. Can smell the beasts a mile away. This is going to add to the fun," she said, clapping her hands in joyful anticipation. "What's his name."

"We don't know," Bliss said, patting the creature on the head as it nudged her thigh for attention. "Mother just sent him over special delivery."

"So what's the bad news?" Tanner asked, seemingly the only one not enamored of the Rapran.

"Jones isn't dead," Port informed them, cutting to the chase.

Stunned, Solace's mouth dropped open in surprise.

"Bliss and I went out early this morning to check for remains in the burned out restroom. It appeared a fire had been started *inside* the building before it took a hit from the first drone missile."

"A fire," she parroted back. "So that's the heat it saw and what the drone targeted. The fire drew its attention, not body heat from Jones."

"Bingo," Port said. "But he must have been wounded on the first fly by from the drone, and somehow while starting the building on fire, he was burned, too. We found footprints, scraps of burnt hair and a green blood trail leading away from the area into the rocky hillside opposite the valley."

"The prints eventually turned from Hume-shaped to Rep," Bliss added. "That's when we lost him, and there are caves up there, deep enough and big enough for him to hideout, shielding his body heat as he licks his wounds."

"We gotta get back up there." Solace leaned over and scooped a T-shirt up off the floor.

"Don't you dare get up," Bliss said. "You need your rest."

"I don't think that's what she's been doing in here, Bliss."

"I know Port. I was trying to be tactful."

"Well it sounded more like you were playing the innocent Miss Bliss like when we were young. It still aggravates me."

"You know," Bliss shot back. "I'm the only one who can mind-meld with the Rapran. I could have him chew up your new crossbow if you'd like."

"Settle down you two." Solace dropped the T-shirt and wiggled closer to Tanner. "You're correct. I feel the need for more rest coming on." Under cover of the sheet, she rested one hand low on Tanner's belly.

"Okay, we're out of here," Port said, heading for the door. "We'll go buy food for the critter."

"Good idea. Have fun you guys."

"By the way." Bliss paused, a big smile on her face. "Port didn't like *Winged Fury*. Over used she says, but she agreed we could be the *Sisters of Anu*. Don't you love it?"

Port rolled her eyes. "I had to agree to something, it was the only way to get her off the subject."

Bliss followed Port, and the Rapran followed Bliss.

"Let's buy him a cute little bed and some toys, too."

"Oh brother." Port shook her head and closed the bedroom door.

"Damn it to Europa and back." Solace rolled onto her side and punched the pillow with her fist. "I can't believe that rock-headed piece of scaly dung made it out alive." With an angry growl, she pounded the pillow again.

"Easy babe, we'll find him." Tanner spooned her, wrapping one arm around her waist, holding her tight. "I know what it feels like when a mission doesn't go exactly as planned."

He really did know—another bond between them. A good thing because it made their relationship stronger. But not such a good thing if they couldn't stay together. It would lead to heartache. Yet she could hardly imagine not having him in her future.

"Remember, we're in this for the long haul," he pointed out. "Thanks to you, we won this battle." Pride warmed his words. "And we're going to win this war." The strength and determination in his voice made her believe him.

"Patience isn't my strong suit," she mumbled.

"But persistence is, and that's what will count in the end."

Apparently ready for round two, Tanner's body hardened and beckoned at her backside.

"You're pretty darn persistent yourself," she teased.

As long as the Alpha Warriors were needed here on Earth, she and Tanner could be together. She had to cling to that, make it be enough. Maybe the future would take care of itself. It had often surprised her in the past.

As her temper cooled, her worries scattered, and the rest of her heated up.

Food and the hot tub would have to wait awhile longer.

## *FAE WARRIORS* Glossary of Terms and Places

ATLATL: used to increase the leverage in throwing a spear. It is the first compound weapon.

ANIME: Japanese Adventure Cartoons

AQUEOUS II: a training planet

CARONIUM: planet where the purest gold in the Multiverse is mined

CARPATHENA: planet of the yogi masters

CETI 9: home of the Manshees

CRONOS 12: where the male Fae Warriors are fighting Out-worlders

CRYSTAL COSMOS NO. 5: Solace's favorite perfume

DARRIUS III: planet of the salt fields

DARRIUS VI: planet of the Crap-eater Megaderms

EPSILON-B: planet of ice caves.

EXOSPHERE: The outermost region of the earth's atmosphere

KEPLER 186F: the Fae Warriors' home planet

LIGHT-YEAR: the distance that light travels in one year. (Nearly 6 trillion miles).

MERCURY: Mother's messenger "boy" and lover

MILESIANS: the ancestors of the modern Irish

METROSEXUAL: Metropolitan heterosexual

NANOSECOND: one billionth of a second.

OUT-WORLDERS: those beyond the home galaxy

PARADISE III: a recreational planet

PARSEC: 3.26 light years

RAPRAN: companion animal, looks half mastiff and half Bengal tiger, with a touch of kangaroo.

REMEDIUM 5: a healing planet

RIGEL 5: the prison planet

SATURNALIA CREAM: made on the home planet for

soothing bruises and wounds

TERAHEATHAN PLANET: known for art and spun glass

THE DRAGON LORDS OF ANU: the offspring of the fallen angels (Anunnaki)

THE SISTERS OF ANU: Bliss' super hero name for the three sisters

TUATHA DE DANANN: the people of the goddess, ancestors to the Fae

*A sneak peek:*

# Bliss

## by

# Gini Rifkin

*Fae Warriors, Book 2*

*Late summer, Boulder, Colorado*

Noodge pulled against his collar nearly jerking the leash from Bliss' hand. Her beloved Rapran was on the trail of something big, yet as she scoped out the dog park, her Fae senses didn't detect anything amiss.

Almost an hour until sunrise, there were no humans to be seen—even the squirrels appeared to still be asleep. Bliss enjoyed the early morning quiet, and it was the only time she could walk the creature without causing a ruckus or being caught by the Animal Control lady.

The unrelenting woman patrolled the area like a prison exercise yard, and they'd already had two narrow escapes.

"Slow down, Noodge," she ordered, but the command seemed to fall on big furry deaf ears.

Her Fae Warrior sisters, Solace and Portence loved Noodge too, but only Bliss had a modicum of control over him. And she had to admit, the Outer-worldly creature could be a handful. They had trimmed the Rapacious Ranivorous' hair and dyed some of it to a more harmonious color. Now he looked more domesticated, and less like a spectacular combination of Tibetan mastiff, Bengal tiger, and Black-tailed wallaby.

Hanging on for dear life, Bliss flash-moved along behind Noodge as he rocketed out of the park and down the street. They ended up in a blind alley, towering

1

walls of brick surrounding them on three sides. To the right were the backdoors to a beauty parlor and a shoe repair shop. On the left, the kitchen exit to a restaurant/lounge. Noodge snuffled along the ground, his low growly-whine indicating there were Reptiles in the vicinity, or at least one had passed by recently.

What were the Reptiles up to these days? They had been lying low since Solace and her human partner Tanner Jackson had eliminated Mr. Smith. And their adversary, Mr. Jones, had apparently gone underground, relinquishing his swanky office and the fake Priselet Corporation. But no one doubted he would reinvent himself in some other deadly entrepreneurial capacity.

Thank the stars the wave of dead prostitutes had ended with the death of Smith, but now the town seemed plagued by an influx of corrupt gambling practices, sex trafficking, and the selling of illegal drugs.

Noodge stood with his front paws braced up against the wall of the building on the left. Nose in the air, he sniffed and growled.

"Hush, Noodge, be easy," she ordered. "I'll take a look-see, but you mustn't give us away."

This time, the big bundle of hair and heart obediently sat down, head cocked, ears on alert.

Slipping free of her coat, Bliss materialized a small set of utility wings—another blouse ruined as they tore through the cotton material. She needed to speak to Mother Nature about upping her expense account. Levitating, she peeked through the set of high windows. Not much to see. Dimly lit, the room appeared to be an office. A moment later, things got more interesting. A tall figure entered and flipped on a wall switch. As light flooded the room, she drew back slightly.

A hat obscured most of the person's face as he crossed the room to a hulking stand-alone safe wedged into one corner. Fiddling with the dial, he keyed in the combination and shoved the lever downward. Then with obvious effort, he swung wide the thick metal door. The safe was crammed full from top to bottom with money, so tightly stacked she doubted a handful of faerie dust would fit inside.

Liberating a small bundle of bills, he ruffled the edges and sniffed at it as if it were a fine wine. Pinot Dinaro, she thought with a giggle. Leaving the safe wide-open, he ambled toward a desk, the money cradled in his arm. Halfway there, he took off his hat and tossed it Frisbee style onto a chair. Along with a smug smile, the nasty scars on his neck and left cheek were revealed. The disfigurement appeared to be from burns, the marks running upward onto his head— leaving his short hair spotty and unattractive. Scars or no scars, she still recognized the scaly wretch. It was Mr. Jones himself, in his human form.

She jerked away in surprise, smacking her left knee against the brick wall. It hadn't taken him long to heal sufficiently enough to be out and about, but then reptiles were like that, and could even regrow appendages, other than their heads. Apparently they weren't as good at re-growing hair.

She stared down at Noodge. Tongue lolling, tail wagging, he pranced back and forth from one front paw to the other. He looked so innocent, but when so ordered, his playful attitude could turn to death-dealing aggression. *Good boy. You earned your keep today,* she mentally praised, longing to add a tummy rub and a pat on the head. His tracking down Jones should squash any doubts about keeping the big unruly animal around.

Studying Jones, she checked the urge to morph into warrior mode. If there were other Reps in the building, things could get messy. But Noodge wasn't far enough along in his training to send him off for help. To be honest, even leaving him here in stakeout mode sounded chancy. She closed her eyes and tried summoning her sisters. No luck. Eyes open, she glanced around. The canyon-like walls of solid-brick were blocking her connection. If she gained elevation, higher than the rooftops, maybe—

"There you are, you mangy interloper." Tranq gun strapped to her hip, the Animal Control woman hustled down the alleyway waving her ticket book like a battle flag. "I thought that was you in the park. And no tags on your collar. You won't get away this time."

Holy Hector, they'd been had. Noodge gave a roar, ending in his usual bloodcurdling howl. That gave the woman pause. It also garnered Mr. Jones' attention, and the window beside her creaked open. Bliss shot straight up onto the roof and peered over the gutter.

"What's going on down there," Jones groused, hanging out far enough for her to see the top of his mutilated head.

"Don't worry mister," the woman called up to him. "I got this handled." Having an audience seemed to spur the stalwart but foolish woman into action, and she went for the tranq gun.

Bliss wasn't about to let Noodge be hurt or captured, although the dose the woman carried would most likely only irritate Noodge, leading to more chaos.

The woman had picked the wrong pooch to pinch.

Cloaking her image, Bliss launched herself off the roof, and swooping downward on a fly-by, knocked the tranq gun out of the woman's hand. Then she hovered and waited, sending a mental command for Noodge to stay in position. The woman spun around, looking first one way and then the other, anger and confusion contorting her features. Bliss glanced up at the window. Jones was gone. The Reps were familiar with Raprans. Had he recognized Noodge as being one? They needed to get out of here pronto.

Just as she mentally told Noodge to come, the overzealous woman grabbed a broken mop handle from a nearby dumpster and took a swing at him. Holy Helios. This broad was crazy. The Rapran easily scrambled out of the way and turning held his ground. The woman had more balls than brains, in this case a possibly lethal combination.

Bliss caught the woman from behind and shoved her halfway across the alley. But before she could abscond with Noodge, a movement up the passageway toward the street, and their only way out, grabbed her attention. There would be no avoiding a fight now.

Blushed with the soft light of dawn, the sky shed an ironic rosy glow on the brawny figure as it headed their way. With each step, the image blurred then reconfigure. Thick hair haloed his head—it wasn't Jones. Probably one of his henchmen. His face elongated to accommodate a set of pointy teeth—teeth dripping with saliva as if in anticipation of tasting Fae flesh. Fingernails turned to claws, and a tail appeared. Growing taller by the moment, his clothes became shreds and fell away as shiny scales shingled the muscular body revealed.

Bliss dropped her cover and landed near Noodge. Upgrading her wings to metal-tipped battle category, she drew her laser gun and took aim. The Animal Control woman groaned and started to get up. "Stay put," Bliss ordered, but the disagreeable woman didn't listen. She clamored forward, blocking a clear shot.

The Rep, in all its hideous glory, kept on coming, closing fast. Not missing a step, he backhanded the obstinate woman out of the way, sending her crashing against the brick and mortar. A bloody streak marked the wall behind her as her limp body slid to the ground.

Halting abruptly, the Rep turned and whipped his tail around, scraping up a cloud of dust and trash. Noodge jumped over the deadly appendage then leaped on the attacker's back like a lion on a gazelle. A big horrid deadly gazelle not ready to give up the fight.

Again Bliss held her fire, this time not willing to risk hitting Noodge. Crouched and at the ready, she tried not to worry. This is what Raprans were trained for, and they'd learned their lessons well. After Mother Nature had rescued them from torment, she bred the hurt and uncontrollable aggression from them so they could serve the good side, and stand with the Fae Warrior Alpha Team.

Noodge's claws ripped into the Rep's shoulders. Green blood spurted, and a putrid smell overshadowed the other back-alley odors. When Noodge sank his teeth in deep and ripped out the Rep's throat, it was all over but the shouting. Head nearly decapitated, he would bleed out soon, but Bliss had no intention of waiting. They had to get out of here before a crowd gathered or the police showed up.

"Stand down, boy," she ordered Noodge. Then she laser blasted the Rep's head from his body, putting him out of his misery. Not that he deserved mercy. Flash moving over to the Animal Control woman, she checked her neck for a pulse, but found none. She was beyond help. As irritating and uncompromising as the woman had been, she didn't deserve such an ending. No one did.

Wings dematerialized, Bliss and Noodge ran for home.

## A word about the author...

Gini Rifkin lives and plays in Colorado, where she takes in abandoned farm animals. She spent many years with her husband re-enacting the Mountain Man era. Now she volunteers at the local historical society, "love those big hats and long dresses." Her friends and family are her greatest treasure; her animals and her writing, her greatest joy.

www.ginirifkin.com
http://ginirifkin.blogspot.com

~*~

## Other Gini Rifkin titles
## available from The Wild Rose Press, Inc.

*The Dragon and The Rose*
*Lady Gallant*
*Iron Heart*
*Special Delivery*
*Victorian Dream*
*A Cowboy's Fate*

Thank you for purchasing
this publication of The Wild Rose Press, Inc.

If you enjoyed the story, we would appreciate your
letting others know by leaving a review.

For other wonderful stories,
please visit our on-line bookstore at
www.thewildrosepress.com.

For questions or more information
contact us at
info@thewildrosepress.com.

The Wild Rose Press, Inc.
www.thewildrosepress.com

Stay current with The Wild Rose Press, Inc.

Like us on Facebook

https://www.facebook.com/TheWildRosePress

And Follow us on Twitter
https://twitter.com/WildRosePress